P9-BYZ-644

The Chocolate Falcon Fraud

This Large Print Book carries the
Seal of Approval of N.A.V.H.

A CHOCOHOLIC MYSTERY

THE CHOCOLATE FALCON FRAUD

JoANNA CARL

THORNDIKE PRESS

A part of Gale, Cengage Learning

Farmington Hills, Mich • San Francisco • New York • Waterville, Maine
Meriden, Conn • Mason, Ohio • Chicago

GALE
CENGAGE Learning

This is a work of fiction. Names, characters, places, and events either are the product of the author's imagination or are used fictitiously. Any resemblance to actual persons, living or dead, events, or locales is entirely coincidental.

The recipes contained in this book are to be followed exactly as written. The publisher is not responsible for your specific health or allergy needs that may require medical supervision. The publisher is not responsible for any adverse reactions to the recipes contained in this book.

Thorndike Press® Large Print Mystery.
The text of this Large Print edition is unabridged.
Other aspects of the book may vary from the original edition.
Set in 16 pt. Plantin.

LIBRARY OF CONGRESS CATALOGING-IN-PUBLICATION DATA

Names: Carl, JoAnna.
Title: The chocolate falcon fraud : a chocoholic mystery / JoAnna Carl.
Description: Large print edition. | Waterville, Maine : Thorndike Press Large Print, 2016. | © 2015 | Series: A chocoholic mystery | Series: Thorndike Press large print mystery Identifiers: LCCN 2015040228 | ISBN 9781410485489 (hardback) | ISBN 141048548X (hardcover) Subjects: LCSH: Woodyard, Lee McKinney (Fictitious character)—Fiction. | Women detectives—Fiction. | Chocolate industry—Fiction. | Large type books. | BISAC: FICTION / Mystery & Detective / Women Sleuths. | GSAFD: Mystery fiction. Classification: LCC PS3569.A51977 C484 2016 | DDC 813/.54—dc23 LC record available at http://lccn.loc.gov/2015040228

Published in 2016 by arrangement with New American Library, an imprint of Penguin Publishing Group, a division of Penguin Random House LLC

Printed in Mexico
1 2 3 4 5 6 7 20 19 18 17 16

If she's lucky, an author gets a chance to sell a character name. The author doesn't get the money! No, the sale normally benefits some charity, often a literacy or arts fund. In Lawton, Oklahoma, for several years I've been asked to donate a character name to the auction at the Lawton–Fort Sill Arts for All Gala. This event raises money for an umbrella organization supporting visual and performing arts groups. The purchaser of the character name selects a name — his or her own name or that of a special person — which is then used for a character in the book.

Last year's bidding was spirited. Kris and David Gill and Bill and Victoria McCurley combined their bids to make a record high donation for a character name. The donation honored Kris and Bill's mother. So this book is dedicated to —

Mary Kay McCurley,
a lady who loves chocolate and mysteries,

and to

the Lawton-Fort Sill Arts for All,
a group that each year collects and distributes thousands of dollars to support the arts in our community.

ACKNOWLEDGMENTS

This book relied on advice, facts, and information from many people. They included my three children — Ruth Henson, Betsy Peters, and John Sandstrom — each of whom has a skill set that's a major help to a mystery-writing mom. I also relied on Elizabeth Garber, of Best Chocolate in Town in Indianapolis; Tom Bolhuis, a pro at boat building and restoration at Great Lakes Boating; Deborah Baroff, head curator of the Museum of the Great Plains; lawman Jim Avance; Dr. Rosemary Bellino; Dr. Nils Axelsen; Tim Raubinger and Jack Cooper. Additional help came from Michigan friends Tracy Paquin, Susan McDermott, and Judy Hallisy.

I'm sure that fans of noir films hold get-togethers at which they dress in costumes, portray famous detectives and gangsters, trade souvenirs and memorabilia, and otherwise, well, behave like fans. A cursory search of the Internet, however, did not reveal a lot of information about these events. Therefore, I felt free to create my own world of noir fandom.

JoAnna Carl

Chapter 1

When Jeff Godfrey came in the door of TenHuis Chocolade, I didn't know if I should shake his hand, kiss him, or call the cops.

My relationship with Jeff was closer than handshaking — or it had been — but not as close as kissing. And the last time I saw Jeff, he'd barely escaped being accused of murder.

Of course, I had to look at Jeff closely before I was sure who he was; I hadn't seen him in three and a half years. Now, at twenty-two, Jeff looked quite different. More mature, of course, but also more handsome and more confident. And he'd gotten rid of the enormous eyelets in his earlobes.

So when he appeared, I stared for a moment. Then I called out, "Jeff! What are you doing there? I mean, here!"

Jeff grinned shyly as he walked across the

shop. He probably felt as ill at ease as I did. By the time I was standing up, leaning against my desk, he was beside me. We settled for the handshake-chest-bump-air-kiss ritual, as if one of us were a talk show host and the other a featured guest.

I motioned him into the chair on the other side of my desk and sat back down. "You look great," I said. "Let me guess — you're here for this weekend's film noir festival, aren't you?"

"That's right. I read about it online. How could I pass up the lectures on *The Maltese Falcon*?"

The Warner Pier Film Festival was always a big success at increasing our tourist traffic. And this year, as a member of the Chamber of Commerce Tourism Committee, I was even invited to the big kickoff party at the yacht club. "And how are your folks?"

"Well, they're still together — again. And you married that Joe guy, right? The boat builder?"

"Yep. We seem to have gotten it right this time. And Joe's now just a boat builder part-time. He's back in the lawyer game three days a week. How about Tess? Do you still see her?" Tess had figured importantly in Jeff's life four years earlier.

"Tess and I see each other on campus. And she works part-time for my dad."

I realized I was beaming, and that Jeff was looking pleased, too. That made me beam even harder. After all, not every ex-stepson is happy to see his ex-stepmother.

I'm Lee McKinney Woodyard, and four years earlier I had moved from Dallas to Warner Pier, Michigan, the most picturesque resort town on Lake Michigan. Here I was business manager for a luxury chocolate company owned by my aunt, Nettie TenHuis Jones.

One reason I'd made the move was to cut all ties with Jeff's dad, my ex-husband. But I still liked his son.

Jeff did look great. At eighteen he'd been a scrawny kid with gray hair, blue eyes, and an enormous hole in each earlobe. He'd also had a gold ring in his left eyebrow, and he'd worn thick glasses.

Now he was at least two inches taller — I guessed his new height at six feet — and thirty pounds more muscular. He'd definitely lost the scrawny teenage look, and he'd also lost the piercings and the glasses. I could barely see the scars where the earlobes had been repaired. He blinked, and I diagnosed contact lenses. Instead of ragged jeans, he was wearing a brand-name polo, khakis, and boat shoes. The result was a great-looking guy.

I counted mentally. Yes, Jeff would have been a senior at Southern Methodist University this year. "Did you just graduate?"

"Yep, I squeaked through. BA in history. And I even got into graduate school at UT."

University of Texas; all of us Texans know those initials. "Wonderful! What's your field?"

"Maybe Texas history. I think I want to teach. I got a slot as a graduate assistant. And I had an offer of an internship at the Texas Museum of Popular Culture. I had to turn that down because I had a conflict."

"That's still great." I leaned toward Jeff and dropped my voice. "What does your dad think of a history career?"

He laughed. "He'd rather I got an MBA, of course, but he said he'd pay my grad school tuition and books."

"He's proud of you, Jeff."

"Maybe. Most of the time he hides it. He'd still like me to sell real estate."

"Do your own thing." I shook a finger at him. "I'm really tickled to see you. Joe and I live in the old cottage now. I hope you'll stay with us."

Jeff straightened his shoulders a little. "Thanks, but I already have a hotel room.

I'm actually doing a research project this trip. Warner Pier was all booked up, but I've got a room in Holland. And I hope you and Joe — and Aunt Nettie and her husband, too — will let me take you all out to dinner tonight."

I knew Aunt Nettie would want to cook for Jeff — she wants to feed the whole world — but I could see Jeff was spreading his grown-up wings a little. I assured him we'd all love to be his guests.

"And I can legitimately write it off as part of my research," Jeff said.

"What are you residing? I mean, researching?" Yikes! I'd pulled another one of my tongue twisters.

Jeff didn't react to it. "Did you ever hear of anybody around here named Fal-cone? Or Fal-cone-ie? I'm not sure of the pronunciation."

"Sounds too Italian for Warner Pier. You know nearly everybody around here is Dutch."

I picked up the phone book and thumbed through, hunting for the *F* listings, but Jeff stood up. "I already checked the directories and the Internet. No person or business with that name is listed."

"We can ask Aunt Nettie. She knows more people than I do. She's in Holland for a dental appointment. She'll want to see you as soon as she gets back."

"She was so nice to me. Before. Is the Inn on the Pier still a good place to eat?"

"Sure."

"Seven o'clock?"

"That sounds fine."

"See you there."

We exchanged cell phone numbers, and I added a warning. "Big areas around here still have no cell service. Including our house. The only place Joe and I have reception — most of the time — is on the roof! They blame the lake, but I have my doubts. They put a tower on one of the highest spots in Saugatuck and reception around there improved dramatically." I stood up. "Wait a minute, and I'll walk you to the door."

I reached for my crutch. For the first time Jeff saw that and my orthopedic boot.

"Hey, Lee! What have you done to yourself?"

"Nothing serious. I sprained an ankle on those steep stairs at the house. I'm sure you remember them."

Jeff nodded. He'd slept in an upstairs bedroom on his previous visit to Warner Pier, and once or twice he had nearly fallen down our steep stairs himself.

"They tell me no permanent damage has been done," I said, "but the doctor wants me to keep weight off the ankle for a while."

I stumped along behind Jeff as we passed through our retail shop, and I insisted he select a chocolate. He went for a dark chocolate falcon, a two-inch replica of the famous film bird that we had created especially for the film festival.

When we reached the street door, we did our belly-bump-air-kiss-hug act again.

"Seven o'clock," Jeff said.

"Seven o'clock," I answered.

And at seven o'clock four of us — my husband, Joe; my aunt Nettie; her husband, Police Chief Hogan Jones; and me — met in the bar at the Inn on the Pier, ready to have dinner with Jeff. I had told everyone how good he had looked, how mature he had seemed, and how pleased he had been at the prospect of seeing all of us again.

So it was quite a letdown when he didn't show up.

We waited in the bar until eight o'clock. I knew, because I checked my watch — again — the third time the hostess came to tell us we could have a table.

"I don't understand this," I said. "I can call Jeff's cell phone again."

"Let's take this table in any case," Hogan said. "Dinner will be my treat."

Aunt Nettie looked worried. She had beautiful curly white hair and a sweet face. "I'm afraid something has happened to Jeff."

Joe laughed. "Something has! He's run into someone more interesting. Despite the changes in his appearance, Lee, I'm afraid Jeff is still the irresponsible kid who showed up on your roof nearly four years ago and tried to break in through the upstairs window."

"Hand me my crutch," I said. "Once we're seated, I'll try his cell phone again."

But there was still no answer.

Hogan left his menu closed and began to make noises like a cop. "Do you know where Jeff was staying?"

"A Holland motel."

"That narrows it down to maybe fifty, sixty places. Does he have your cell phone number?"

I nodded.

"Did he say why he came to Warner Pier?"

"He said he was going to catch part of the film festival, and that he was doing a research project. But he didn't explain anything about it. He asked me if I knew anyone named Fal-cone or Fal-cone-ie. He wasn't sure of the pronunciation."

"Falconi?" Aunt Nettie looked surprised. "That would be an odd name around Warner Pier. Valk, maybe."

Valk? What could Valk have to do with Falcone? I started to ask Aunt Nettie to explain, but the waiter interrupted. We all put our attention on the menus, and after we had ordered dinner some unwritten rule of good manners inspired us to stop discussing Jeff.

But why had Jeff invited us all to dinner, then failed to show up? I had no explanation. But then, maybe I didn't know Jeff all that well.

His parents, Dina and Rich, had divorced when Jeff was nine. Three years later I married Rich, who was then in his early forties. I was twenty-three. Dumb. Dumb. Dumb. Marrying Rich was the stupidest thing I ever did, though the age difference was the least of our problems.

Today I understood that I fell for Rich because I wanted stability in my life. He fell for me because I was six feet tall and a natural blond who had been in a Miss Texas competition.

Also, I think, he liked me because I have malapropism. This means I get my tongue twisted, saying such things as "residing" when I mean "researching," as I did when talking to Jeff. Rich thought "dumb" and "blond" were synonyms, and he didn't want any mental competition from his wife. He loved it when I goofed.

In those days Jeff was a bratty adolescent. Rich had his custody one or two weekends a month and on some holidays. Or maybe I had his custody. Rich was a successful real estate developer in Dallas, and he often managed to be playing golf with a client at the times when he should have been paying attention to Jeff. I will say he was careful not to miss any of Jeff's swim meets. The kid could swim and dive like a dolphin.

There's a fine line between getting along with an adolescent and keeping one from bossing you around. Jeff was a nice enough kid, but dealing with a stepmother who was only eleven years older than he was — well, it wasn't an ideal situation for either of us.

After some sparring around, Jeff and I developed an informal truce. We spent a lot of time on neutral activities such as playing board games and watching old movies. Even in those days Jeff was a fan of forties and fifties noir films and books.

For five years I struggled to make my marriage work. But my relationship with Rich got worse and worse. I wanted to think of marriage as a partnership. Rich wanted to think of me as a possession. I'd become the proverbial trophy wife, and I didn't like it. And I couldn't get Rich even to discuss the situation.

Finally I left, and I didn't take anything with me. I abandoned my jewelry (selected by Rich), my snazzy car (picked out by Rich), my elegant house (gussied up by a decorator Rich chose), even my wardrobe (though Rich had allowed me to pick out my own clothes, provided I went to the stores he approved of).

When I left Rich I drove away in a junky car somebody had abandoned at my dad's garage. I was wearing an old pair of jeans and a T-shirt. I moved in with my mom, who was on Rich's side, and I begged until she bought me a tank of gas. Then I took a job as a waitress because I could start work that day and keep my tips.

My plan was to convince Rich that I loved *him,* not his money, and thus save my marriage. This did not work. It took a couple of months with a counselor for me to understand that Rich regarded his money as part of his personality. In rejecting it, I had rejected him.

When I discovered Rich had put detectives on my trail, I accepted the end of my marriage. I wasn't seeing anyone else, but Rich couldn't believe I'd leave one wealthy man without having a new one lined up.

About the time my marriage ended, my wonderful aunt Nettie — world's finest chocolatier — offered me a job as business manager of TenHuis Chocolade. I moved to Warner Pier. I met Joe Woodyard — who had also had some unhappy romantic times. Now we'd been married three years. And I loved my life.

But apparently my decision to get a divorce brought a personality crisis for Rich. He went into counseling and must have done a lot of self-examination. Then he began to see Dina again. A year and a half after our divorce, the two of them remarried.

I wished them all sorts of happiness. But that part of my life was over. I didn't want to see them ever again. However, I could hardly refuse to meet with Jeff. He and I had watched a lot of Humphrey Bogart and Alan Ladd.

But why had Jeff invited us all to dinner, then failed to show?

I went to bed that night puzzled by Jeff's nonappearance, but trying not to worry about him. Unfortunately the scrabbling of my thoughts was echoed by some darn animal making noises in the attic (a chronic problem of semirural living) and I had trouble falling asleep. I insisted to myself that Joe was right; Jeff had simply found someone more interesting to have dinner with. I shouldn't be wringing my hands over him.

I was still sleeping when the phone rang at seven the next morning. Joe was already awake, and he answered it.

"Oh, hi." He sounded wary. "Sure. She's here."

Where else would I be at that time of day? I took the phone and mumbled my greeting. "It's Lee."

"Lee, it's Alicia."

"Alicia?" I sat up in bed. I had recognized the Texas accent immediately. "Alicia Richardson!"

"Oh yeah. The same old gal. How you doin'?"

"Fine! It's good to hear from you."

And it was good. Alicia was a part of my life in Dallas I remembered with pleasure. At one time she'd helped me out a lot.

Alicia was office manager and head of accounting for Rich's company. I guess every business has one key person, and at Godfrey Development, Alicia was it. She had worked for Rich for at least fifteen years. She knew where all the bodies were buried, where all the money was socked away, who couldn't stand whom, and how to Get Things Done.

On a day-to-day basis, Alicia ran the company. Rich made the deals, and Alicia made them happen. Rich didn't admit this out loud, but the salary he paid Alicia proved he appreciated her abilities. Their relationship was strictly professional. Alicia was married to a terrific guy named Tom who was a surveyor, and they had two great kids. She was perfectly capable of telling Rich she couldn't stay late because it was her daughter's birthday, and Rich would say, "Yes, ma'am."

Back when I was married to Rich, Alicia had saved my fanny lots of times. If Rich and I were going to a party, for example, she'd give me tips on what was really going on in the world of property development, and which subjects to avoid with whom. She kept my foot out of my mouth most of the time.

If I had a role model in my job as business manager for TenHuis Chocolade, it was Alicia. I was glad to hear from her, though I knew she hadn't called simply to chat.

Sure enough, she went right to the point.

"I don't suppose you've heard from Jeff," she said. "That little booger seems to have misplaced hisself."

Chapter 2

"Misplaced himself? Alicia, I thought he finally grew up enough to be allowed out of the house alone."

"As a general rule he does pretty well. But his parents are in South America until the end of the week, and something has come up. He mentioned you before he got away."

"Actually Jeff did drop by yesterday."

Alicia gave a dramatic sigh of relief. "Thank the Lord! Is he there with you?"

"No, he said he had a motel room in Holland."

"Was he okay?"

"Sure. He looked great and seemed to be in good spirits." My mind was racing, and fear was settling in the pit of my stomach. It was stupid, but I'd always had a terrible fear that something would happen to Jeff and that it would happen on my watch.

But what should I say to Alicia? Jeff had made a date with us, then had failed to show up. Should I tell her that? I stalled.

"I guess he told you he was common — I mean, coming! He must have told you he was coming to Warner Pier."

"No, he didn't tell me! He's living at home this summer. He gave up his apartment, because he's going to move to Austin in August. Rich and Dina are skiing, of all things, in Peru, of all places. Jeff was supposed to mind his mama's store."

Dina owned a high-end antiques business, and Jeff had worked part-time for her since he was fourteen or so.

Alicia was still talking. "He found someone to fill in at the store, then went off — I guess to Michigan — and apparently didn't tell anybody where he was going. Not even that sweet little Tess. I finally found a message from him on my line at the office. It said something about seeing you. And he's not answering his cell phone. Do you know what motel he's in?"

"I'm afraid not. All he gave me was his cell number."

"Dadgum it!"

"Alicia, is there some emergency?"

"I honestly don't know, Lee. The girl who's at Dina's shop called me to say Jeff was getting these strange phone calls. I went over there and listened to a couple of messages, and, Lee, they sound a lot like threats! Like 'If you miss this opportunity, you'll be sorry forever, because the black bird may come after you.' "

"Who on earth would threaten Jeff?"

"I can't imagine. I don't know what's going on. But I need to talk to him about it. If anything happens to Jeff . . ." She left the sentence incomplete.

I decided that I wouldn't tell Alicia about Jeff being a no-show for dinner. She was worried already, and that wouldn't help.

"Listen," I said, "as soon as I'm a little more up-and-at-'em, I'll get on the phone and call a few Holland motels. Maybe I can track him down."

"Oh, would you? I'd really appreciate it."

Alicia gave me her cell number, and I promised to call back by noon, even if I didn't find Jeff.

I hung up, then slumped down in bed and looked at Joe. Darn, he was fun to look at. Dark hair, brilliant blue eyes. Definitely the best-looking guy in west Michigan. With the best shoulders. Also smart.

"Good morning," I said.

Joe rolled his eyes. "Why do your friends and relatives call so early?"

"They forget we're in the eastern time zone."

"But that would make them call later, Lee. Not earlier."

"Then I don't know. But you were already up. Why did the phone bother you?"

"I guess I just don't like to see you get mixed up with those people."

"What's wrong with Alicia and Jeff? At least *Rich* didn't call."

"He doesn't bother me. You're not friendly with Rich. It's other people who want favors."

"I haven't heard from any of them since Jeff got in all that trouble on his last visit. Three years ago. Three and a half."

"But yesterday, when he showed up, you said Jeff knew we were married."

"Yes, and he knew Aunt Nettie and Hogan were married. So what? Oh, it's odd, because he didn't get it from me."

"He's been keeping track of you, Lee. It's creepy. Plus, last night you and Aunt Nettie were talking about meeting with that architect today. You don't have time to look all over Holland for Jeff."

TenHuis Chocolade ("luxury chocolates in the Dutch tradition") had recently acquired the building next door. We were in the early stages of expanding into the additional space. Even the early stages were taking a lot of time.

I sighed. "Joe, I can't refuse to help Alicia find Jeff. She's obviously worried about him. And Alicia is one of those people I owe."

I sat up and rested my chin on my knees. "This is one of those recurring nightmares."

"Why? I'm sure nothing's happened to Jeff."

"It's a holdover from when I was first married to Rich. I admit we hadn't dated nearly long enough. He hadn't bothered to mention that he had a twelve-year-old son."

"What a jerk!"

"True, but . . . Anyway, a month after I met Jeff, Rich asked me to pick him up for weekend visitation and bring him out to the club and drop him off to have dinner with Rich. I had to go someplace else. So I took Jeff to the club and dropped him off at the front door. I had barely gotten where I was going when Rich called and asked where Jeff was. He'd never gotten inside the club."

"That was scary!"

I blinked away a tear. "Actually he'd just gone out to the driving range, but it frightened the something or other out of me. All I could think was that he'd been kidnapped. And it would all be my fault!"

Joe sat on the edge of the bed and took my hand. "Jeff's a grown-up now!"

"Is he?"

"Legally he is. You didn't ask him to come to Michigan. He's responsible for himself."

"Thanks, but this is a topic I'm not always rational about."

Joe gave me a kiss and another dose of reassurance. Then I got up, hoisted myself onto my crutch, and limped through my morning routine. As soon as Joe left for work, I started calling motels in Holland, thirty miles away, looking for Jeff. It only took four calls. He was registered at the Holiday Inn Express.

But when the front desk rang his room, Jeff didn't answer. I left a voice mail, telling him Alicia was trying to find him. And I added a sentence. "We were sorry that we missed you last night, Jeff. Don't leave the area without calling, guy!"

I began to dress for the office, telling myself I'd hear from Jeff within a few minutes. He had probably been in the shower.

But I didn't hear from him. By the time I left for the office, thumping my crutch irately at every step, there had been no word from Jeff.

After Joe left, the only sound I heard was the animal in the attic.

Anyone who's ever lived in the country

knows about the animal in the attic. And if Joe and I didn't live in the country in a legal sense, we did in a physical one. Our house was inside the city limits of Warner Pier. We had city water and sewer, plus all the police and fire protection available in a town of twenty-five hundred souls. But our neighborhood was semirural and heavily wooded. It looked and felt like country. We were surrounded by country things like bushes and trees and animals.

Deer, turkeys, raccoons, rabbits — even the occasional badger and fox — hung out in our neighborhood. And they considered our house part of their territory. A squirrel had come down our chimney. We'd had chipmunks move into our basement. Every fall the mice invaded, trying to avoid cold weather. Don't ask me how they found cracks and holes to get in; we tried to plug 'em up.

We were experts on amateur extermination, and we also knew whom to call if professional action was required. In fact, we'd had the exterminator the previous week, and he thought he had de-animaled the house completely. But I was already hearing noises from the attic.

This situation, of course, was not found only in Michigan. My dad had the same problem in north Texas. It's just part of country living, so we tried not to pay too much attention to stray scratchings and thumpings.

But I wrote a note to Joe with a big, fat Magic Marker. "Please check attic for annie-mule!" Then I taped it to the window over the kitchen sink before I left for the office.

I made sure my phone was on; I didn't want to miss Jeff's call. But by noon I still hadn't heard from him. When I talked to Alicia, she hadn't heard from him either.

"Listen," I said, "I'll go to the Holiday Inn and see what I can find out."

"If that kid is lounging around the pool and letting us worry, I'll have his hide."

"I'll hold him while you kick him."

I told Aunt Nettie I was making an emergency trip to Holland and would be back to meet with the architect. I worried the whole thirty miles to Holland. But I was on the outskirts of town before I gave in, stopped the car in a parking lot, and called Hogan for a little informal advice from law enforcement. Luckily it was a slow day for crime in Warner Pier, and I caught him in his office.

I quickly sketched the situation for him. "We can't make a missing person report on Jeff yet, can we?"

"Not unless you find something scary."

"Scary?"

"Yeah. Like his car with a pool of blood in the front seat."

I shuddered. "I don't even want to think such a thing!"

"Then don't. But if he's simply not there, the cops can't do much. He's over twenty-one, isn't he?"

"Oh yes. He's supposedly a grown-up."

"And the motel isn't likely to give you much information."

"That's what I thought."

"The only way you could get a look in his room, for example, is if there was a possibility he's sick."

"Sick?"

"Some chronic condition. The possibility of a diabetic coma maybe. He's a little bit young for you to tell them he might have had a stroke. And you don't want to say he'd threatened suicide. The motel might toss him out. Motels don't like dead guests." Hogan laughed. "But don't make it too elaborate, Lee. You don't look old enough to be Jeff's mother."

"Even though I was. Sort of."

When I got to the Holiday Inn I cruised the parking lot, looking for Texas license plates. Nary a one. So I parked and went to the desk, where the clerk tried calling Jeff's room. No answer.

I took a deep breath and pulled the stunt Hogan had hinted might work.

My stepson, I told the clerk, was diabetic. "We really didn't want him to tackle this trip, because his blood sugar has been up and down, but you know kids! We couldn't talk him out of it."

The clerk nodded sympathetically.

"Is there any way a staff member could check the room? Make sure he's all right?"

"I'll ask the manager."

The manager wasn't happy, but he got a special key card from a drawer. I didn't ask if I could go along. I just went.

The room was on the third floor. I tried to follow the manager inside, but he gestured at me. "Please stay here."

So I stood in the doorway, though I did manage to edge inside far enough to see into the bathroom and most of the bedroom. By then I had talked myself into real concern about Jeff's disappearance, and I was holding my breath as the manager made a circuit of the room, checking behind the shower curtain, between the beds, in the closet. I felt a genuine sense of relief when he spoke. "No sign of him."

"Thank goodness." From my place two

steps inside the room I could see Jeff's luggage — a medium-sized wheeled duffel bag — on the foot of the bed. I could peek inside the bathroom and see his shaving kit on the counter. But neither bag looked as if it had been opened.

Jeff had apparently checked in the previous day, dropped off his luggage, then left. There was no sign that he had ever come back to the room.

The manager relocked the door, and I followed him downstairs. He seemed even more relieved than I was, and I could understand why. As Hogan had said, motels don't like dead guests.

When we returned to the front desk, I tried one more thing. "Do I need to give you a credit card? To make sure Jeff's room is paid for?"

Then the manager *did* look relieved. To learn that some family member was willing to pick up Jeff's bill — he practically clicked his heels. But he assured me that Jeff had a credit card on file. All was well.

"I'll just call his mother," I said.

The manager frowned. "I thought you were his mother."

I chuckled. "No, his stepmother. We're a blended family." I ended with another chuckle.

That reassured him, and he didn't make any objection when I helped myself to a cup of their free coffee, then took a seat in the empty breakfast area. I took out my phone.

And Tess walked in the front door of the motel.

Chapter 3

At least I thought it was Tess. Like Jeff, she was almost four years older than the last time I'd seen her, and like him, she had changed in the years between eighteen and twenty-two.

The girl approaching the registration desk was tiny — I'd guess her jeans at size zero — with dark hair in a wispy haircut. She used quick, birdlike gestures that reminded me of the Tess I'd met three and a half years earlier. I stood up, more and more confident that this was Tess.

She had a clear, high-pitched voice. From thirty feet away I could understand what she asked the clerk.

"Do y'all have a Jeff Godfrey registered here?"

It was definitely Tess.

The clerk, understandably, looked surprised. Jeff Godfrey must be her most popular guest that afternoon. She hesitated, and her eyes flickered in my direction.

Tess spoke again. "Jeffrey Godfrey? Or J. A. Godfrey? From Dallas, Texas?"

I decided to let the clerk off the hook. "Tess! Tess! I didn't know you came to Michigan, too."

I would say that Tess looked happy to see me. And I was truly happy to see her. Tess was a close friend of Jeff's. She was a sweet girl, and she was sure to know how to contact Jeff.

Tess came over, and we exchanged big Texas hugs. I had to lean way over, since I was close to a foot taller than Tess, but I managed to handle my crutch. At least I didn't fall over, and I gave a brief explanation of my injury, assuring her it was minor.

For a few minutes, we went on gushing the way Texas girls do. Tess told me she had finished at SMU a month earlier, earning a degree in sociology. Like Jeff, she was to enter graduate school at the University of Texas in August.

Then I got another hug. "Oh, Lee! I'm so glad to see you!" Tess stood back and looked all around the lobby. And she dropped a little bombshell.

"Where's Jeff?" she asked.

My heart sank to my knees. "Oh no! Tess, I was sure you'd know where he is. I'm looking for him, and Alicia — I'm sure you know Alicia — is looking for him frantically."

Tess rolled her eyes. "Jeff might not answer her calls."

"He hasn't been answering mine either."

"He usually picks up for me."

We sat down in the breakfast area, and she pulled out a cell phone in a cute zebra-striped case. She smiled complacently as she called up her contacts list, and she winked at me as she punched the phone.

"I'll find out where that bad boy is," she said.

Her smile slowly faded as she waited. And waited. I could hear the rings. Five of them. Then I heard Jeff's voice. "Please leave a message after the beep."

"He's not answering," she said. "I'll *get* him!"

I looked at my watch. I needed to leave for Warner Pier within fifteen minutes. I had to try to find out what was going on in that time.

"Tess," I asked, "what are you and Jeff up to?"

"Up to?" Tess' eyes and voice were as innocent as the proverbial newborn babe.

I steeled my resolve. "Yes, Tess. Why have the two of you come to Michigan? You're not in some weird kind of trouble again?"

"Oh no, Lee!" Tess giggled. "It's nothing *serious*! Jeff doesn't even know I'm here. Anyway, it's just a game."

"What kind of a game?"

"Well . . ."

I made my voice stern. "I have to be back in Warner Pier in forty-five minutes. I don't have time to beg. You've got to tell me. And Alicia Richardson better not have been bugging me all morning over a game."

"Oh, Lee. It's going to seem silly to you, but it's real important to Jeff. And to me. See, we've both been interns at the Texas Museum of Popular Culture, the Dallas branch. And they're having a competition. Film collectibles. Noir nostalgia."

"Noir nostalgia? As in noir films?"

"Right! I knew you'd understand."

"I understand what a noir film is. The Warner Pier Film Festival is saluting noir movies this summer. But what's the museum competition about?"

"Memorabilia. The person who brings in the most significant piece of noir memorabilia wins a prize. Five thousand dollars."

"Five thousand dollars! Where is a museum getting that kind of money?"

"It's a grant. From the Grossman Foundation."

"And what is the Grossman Foundation?" I asked the question, then realized I was getting off the subject. "Never mind that," I said. "Did you and Jeff both come up here on the trail of some movie souvenir?"

"Sort of. I admit I followed Jeff. But I also came because of the Warner Pier Film Festival. Lots of collectors and traders are going to be here. Jeff came because he heard about something that he thought might really take the prize."

"What was it?"

"Something to do with *The Maltese Falcon.*" Her gaze wavered again.

I decided to let her off the hook. "Never mind. It wouldn't mean anything to me." I checked the time again. "Tess, Joe and I are living in the old cottage where you stayed with Aunt Nettie and me. We've even put in a second bathroom! Upstairs! Why don't you come and stay with us?"

"I don't want to impose. Is Jeff staying there?"

"No, he's registered here. At this motel. But, Tess, grad students are traditionally hard up. I'd hate for you to pay for a motel when you can have a room and private bath with us for free."

She laughed her birdlike laugh. "Okay, Lee. Thanks. I accept."

I quickly wrote out a note giving her directions to our house and to TenHuis Chocolade, since she had made only a brief visit there four years earlier. Then I used my crutch to pull myself to my feet. "Besides, there are some funny things going on, and I'll feel better if you aren't alone up here."

Tess' eyes grew big. "What do you mean?"

"I'm not sure." While we were walking toward the parking lot, I listed the odd things that had happened. Jeff's appearance and disappearance. Alicia's report of strange phone calls. Jeff's checking in to the motel, then never coming back to occupy his room.

"It's not a law enforcement matter yet," I said, "but it's odd. I don't want to misplace you, too."

"I certainly don't want to get misplaced! But can I stop for lunch before I come out?"

"Of course. We're not going to start by starving you. I wish I had time to take you someplace nice. But I've got to get back to TenHuis Chocolade. If you'll come by the shop, I'll give you a key to the house."

Tess and I exchanged cell phone numbers, and I also gave her the numbers for the house and the shop. Then we waved and went our separate ways. I picked up my own lunch at a fast-food drive-through and ate a hamburger on the way out of Holland.

What was I getting into? I'd started out to find Jeff, and I still didn't know where he was. Instead I'd acquired a second stray Texan. I had only a vague idea of why the two of them had turned up in Michigan. Their arrivals apparently had something to do with the Tough Guys and Private Eyes Film Festival and the ultimate noir movie, *The Maltese Falcon.* But I didn't understand what. Between bites of hamburger and slurps of Diet Coke, I began to make mental notes of questions I wanted answered.

Then I told myself I had to postpone that. Instead I had to think about TenHuis Chocolade and our big expansion project. It wasn't off to a very good start.

TenHuis Chocolade had bought the building next door to us five months earlier. A shop specializing in clown paraphernalia and souvenirs had been there for several years. The owner had died — okay, he had been murdered, leaving the building in something of a mess, and his business affairs in an even greater mess. But his heirs had finally cleared everything up, and TenHuis Chocolade had bought the property, a two-story redbrick building from around 1900.

It was typical of buildings in Warner Pier's business district. Quaint but suffering from an awkward update about thirty years earlier. Like most downtown buildings in Warner Pier, it had an apartment upstairs. Joe and I had done a lightning renovation to get that ready to rent.

I believe the word for the building was "ratty." Not that it had rats, of course; we paid an exterminator to make sure it didn't. But the downstairs of the building still looked as if it ought to.

We'd hired an architect to combine our current building and the new one into one beautiful, practical, and unified structure. Of course, the resulting building had to meet the architectural standards of Warner Pier. In other words, it had to look quaint. Everything in our town was supposed to look as if it had been there for at least a century. That was decreed by a city ordinance.

Our architect, Howard Moore, was from Holland and he had already worked on several Warner Pier buildings. So he should understand the city planning and zoning rules. I'd first met him through Joe, who had restored a 1947 Chris Craft for him several years earlier.

I grabbed up a small box of chocolates, and Aunt Nettie and I met Howard outside our "new" old building. Before our discussion began we each had a caramel truffle ("milk chocolate filling covered with milk or dark chocolate and embellished with a contrasting chocolate color swirl"). Business meetings always go better if they start with chocolate.

Howard was in his midforties, with thin hair and a trim build. His most striking feature was a pair of expressive brown eyes. Joe said he suspected that Howard used those eyes to mesmerize clients into accepting his designs.

I'd become a bit surprised at the way Aunt Nettie was handling this project. Usually she was a sweet little lady who never raised her voice, but I'd discovered that when she wanted something, by golly, she wanted it, and she wouldn't back down. And after nearly forty years as a chocolatier, Aunt Nettie knew what she wanted in a chocolate workroom and shop.

So that afternoon Howard, Aunt Nettie, and I spent an hour and a half measuring and discussing space requirements in the building next door. It seemed to me that we kept going over the same things. Aunt Nettie wasn't going to give an inch, and Howard said her ambitions required far too many inches to fit into the available space.

And we hadn't even begun to talk about

what I'd call the "decorative" aspects of the new shop. The old one looked as if it had been decorated in 1950. I wanted something that looked more like 2025. Aunt Nettie didn't seem to care; she was far more interested in the workspace.

I was sure Howard was as frustrated as I was. But Aunt Nettie sailed serenely on, determined to have a model chocolate kitchen.

So I couldn't say I worried about Jeff and Tess that afternoon. I was far too worried about our remodeling project to give them a thought. Besides, I still had confidence that Jeff would turn up perfectly all right, and I had talked Tess into taking shelter under my wing — or at least in one of our upstairs bedrooms.

Of course, Alicia had called three times. Since I had nothing new to tell her, I turned my phone off until I was through wrangling with Howard. If Tess couldn't get through on my cell, she had the shop number.

As Aunt Nettie and I went back to Ten-Huis Chocolade I pictured Tess safe at our house. So I was astonished and upset when I learned Tess had not been by the shop to pick up the house key. I immediately checked my messages. She hadn't called me. Next I called Tess' cell phone, but it immediately went to voice mail.

"Drat the girl!"

Could she have changed her mind and gone back to the Holiday Inn Express? Another phone call eliminated that possibility.

I toyed with checking in with the state troopers to make sure she hadn't had an accident, but I decided that would be overreacting.

I sighed and called Alicia, again telling her that I hadn't heard from Jeff.

"Rich and Dina are on this big Peruvian trip with a bunch of friends," Alicia said. "I can't reach them. And I'm really getting worried. Of course, they're supposed to be home this weekend."

"Let's not panic yet," I said. I tried to make my voice confident. "Surely Jeff will get in touch with one of us tonight."

I hung up, and finally I admitted to myself that I was scared to death. Where could these kids be? I could only hope they were together.

As soon as I got home, I told Joe the whole story.

He just shook his head and assured me Tess and Jeff were all right.

"Tess has found Jeff, and they're playing some game," he said. "Just like she said."

I couldn't say he was wrong, and I hoped he was right.

We had finished dinner, and Joe was promising that he'd check the attic for wildlife when our phone finally rang.

I yanked it up. "Hello."

A weak, frightened little voice spoke my name. "Lee?"

"Tess! Where are you?"

"I'm sorry I didn't get to your house. Things have been really crazy. And now I'm lost."

CHAPTER 4

"Where are you, Tess?"

"I don't know! There's nothing out here but trees."

"What can you see? A gas station? A road sign?"

"Lee, I'm out in the woods on some dirt road! I've been using my GPS, but I guess I got it all confused."

I pressed the speaker button of our phone so that Joe could hear Tess, too. He had grown up in Warner County and seemed to know every back road in southwest Michigan. "What does the GPS say?" I asked.

"It says I'm on Big Pine Road. Does that make sense?"

"There is a Big Pine Road," Joe said. "But it's nowhere near our house. Does the GPS say where you are on Big Pine Road?"

"I can't figure it out. I'm sitting here at a dead end."

Joe's eyes got big. "Good night, Tess!

You're halfway across the county. How'd you get there?"

"I tried to follow directions. I don't know what I did wrong."

"Can you turn the car around and head back the way you came?"

"I can if I'm careful not to get in the ditch."

"So be careful! I remember how narrow that road is. Move only a few feet at a time. Then head back, and stay on that road. Lee and I are on the way to meet you. Hang up now, and we'll call you back as soon as we get cell phone service."

We climbed into Joe's truck and headed east. Within five minutes I had bars on my cell phone and was able to call Tess. This was typical of the cell service near Lake Michigan. And I didn't want one more person to tell me it was caused by the lake. In my opinion, the companies simply wouldn't spend enough money putting up towers. I mean, why should our first floor have had no service, and our second floor a little bit, and the guy who cleaned our chimney be able to call Timbuktu? If we had a tower closer — Oh well.

As we drove, Joe muttered, "I don't see how she managed to get out there."

I covered my phone. "Isn't that near the

dump?"

"It's about five miles past the dump. Tess would have no reason to go out there."

Joe had spoken in a low voice, but apparently Tess heard him. Her voice came over the phone.

"I did have a reason," she said defensively. "I'll tell you when we meet up. I'm turned around now."

"Just go straight back the way you came," Joe said. "Toward the lake."

"No," Tess said. "I'm driving toward the sun, Joe. I'm from Texas. There are a lot of trees out here, but I can still tell where the sun is going down."

At least Tess hadn't lost her sense of humor. When we had met her previously, we had had a discussion about the different concepts of directions. In Texas people were much more likely to say they live "west of town" or "north of Buffalo Hill." Warner Pier folks seemed to orient themselves by Lake Michigan. "Toward the lake" or "inland."

Luckily Tess hadn't gotten herself lost after dark. She'd ended up in a part of the county that was so heavily wooded that she might never have found her way out in the dark.

But she did find her way out. With Tess

headed west — toward the setting sun or the lake — and Joe and me headed east — inland and with the sun behind us — it took us less than fifteen minutes to meet one another. When we finally met up, I switched from Joe's truck to Tess' car, a small red Ford. Joe did the trick of turning around on a narrow dirt road, and Tess and I followed Joe's truck home. Tess didn't volunteer any explanations on the way, and she sure seemed delighted to reach our house.

"We saved a pork chop for you," I said. "I'll heat it up."

"I believe I'm too upset to eat," she said.

"I hope you're not too upset to tell us how you wound up at the end of Big Pine Road," Joe said.

"It's a long story," Tess said. And she ducked her head, almost as if she was ashamed.

What was going on? I decided we'd better go easy on Tess. "Joe will help get your stuff in the house. You can explain after you eat."

But even after Tess had settled into our guest room, and I'd reheated her dinner, she didn't volunteer any information. Finally Joe turned his cross-examination skills loose on her.

"Okay, Tess. How on earth did you wind up way out beyond the township dump?

"I was trying to find Jeff."

"What made you think he was out there?"

"I'm not very good with technology. I guess I messed up the GPS."

"What kind of coordinates did you put into it? Something like 'end of the earth'?"

I thought she might flare up, but Tess just looked shamefaced. "I must have misread the route Jeff took."

"The route Jeff took?" Joe's voice was incredulous. "You thought you were following Jeff?"

Tess nodded miserably.

Joe sighed. "Tess, let's go back a little further. Exactly why did you and Jeff come to Warner Pier? And why didn't you come together? After all, you used to be friends."

Tess smiled. "We still are. But we're also rivals."

She told Joe the story about the contest sponsored by the museum where she and Jeff had been interns.

"Jeff was getting ahead of me," she said. "He found a lead to some new piece of memorabilia to do with *The Maltese Falcon.*"

"A lock of Humphrey Bogart's hair?" I asked. "That movie is so well-known it's hard to think there would be anything new connected with it."

"I don't know what it was. All I know is that Jeff was terribly excited about it. He said that if it was real, it would definitely win the competition."

Joe frowned. "You have no idea what it was?"

"No! I couldn't get a word out of him. Not a hint."

"And he didn't tell you who had it or where it was?"

Tess slowly shook her head. "No. I begged and pleaded. I did Internet searches of my own. I thought I was going to have to give up."

Then she looked up and gave the grin that reminded me she was a cute girl. "Finally," she said, "I stooped to subterfuge."

Joe's eyes narrowed, and I'm sure mine did, too. What had she been up to?

Tess' eyes sparkled. "I went to one of those spy shops. You know, where they sell hidden cameras and phone taps and such. And the day before Jeff left Dallas, I bugged his car."

I looked at Joe, and he looked at me. We both began to laugh. The idea of wide-eyed, innocent Tess in a spy shop was ridiculous.

Then Joe spoke. "A cop would have to get a warrant to do that."

"I'm not a cop. I'm just competitive. I

bought one of those little transmitter thingies. It didn't cost much, because I got a refurbished one. Not new. And I installed it in Jeff's car."

"You installed it in his car?" I was sure I sounded incredulous. "How did you know how to do that?"

"It came with instructions. You plug it in the 'onboard diagnostic port.' " She made air quotes around the phrase. "It doesn't even need batteries."

"Come on, Lee," Joe said. "People install those things all the time so they can tell where their teenagers go. Or keep track of a fleet of delivery trucks. I'm sure the directions are clear."

Tess nodded. "Yep. I'm not at all mechanical, and I handled it. I tracked Jeff all the way to Michigan with my smartphone. But I finally lost him."

"When did that happen?" Joe asked.

"Yesterday afternoon. He went to see Lee." She turned to me. "Didn't he? I saw his car parked in the same block as the chocolate shop."

I nodded. "Jeff didn't stay long. He invited us to dinner, but then he didn't show up. Do you know where he went?"

"I lost him during the afternoon. He began to wander around in all those woods east of Warner Pier. I didn't dare follow too closely, and I got all confused."

Joe grinned. "Did the trees scare you?"

Tess looked puzzled, and I smiled back at Joe as I answered. "The part of Texas where Tess grew up has lots of trees. It's only a plains person like me who's scared of them. Go on, Tess."

She still looked puzzled, but she continued her story. "I finally gave up and came back to Warner Pier. I was watching the tracker on my phone, and it came back to town, too. Then Jeff went down Lake Shore Drive. I thought he was coming here, to your house."

"No sign of him here," I said.

"His car was parked someplace around here for at least an hour. Then it moved back to the area east of Warner Pier, according to the tracking device. And it didn't move again. I looked all around over there, and I didn't find anything likely. I finally decided he'd found the bug and tossed it in the bushes. I had to get a motel in Holland and try again this morning."

"But the bug is still working?" I asked.

Tess nodded. "The location of the bug hasn't changed, and this afternoon I decided I'd try again, make one more effort to track him down. And all that happened was that y'all had to rescue me. I went to the area indicated, but I couldn't find him."

Joe leaned forward. "Was that the end of Big Pine Road?"

"That's how I interpreted the information. But it's just woods out there. There are no roads, no houses. Nothing."

"You ran into the border of a state forest," Joe said absently. "Let me look at your tracker."

Tess dug her smartphone out of her purse, and she showed Joe how the app operated. Joe looked it over. "It seems to be working," he said.

"I probably did something wrong," Tess said.

"Show me."

She demonstrated how she had operated the tracker app. Joe frowned. "That looks right to me," he said. "I'm going to ask Hogan about this."

Joe went into the bedroom to call Hogan. He apparently was told to bring the gadget over. At least he came out of the bedroom and walked swiftly out the back door, headed for his truck. He yelled over his shoulder, "I want to get over to Hogan's before dark!"

I hobbled right after him. "Joe! Joe! What's going on?"

He jumped into the truck and rolled down the window. "Hogan wants to take a look at the tracker right now, Lee."

"Why the hurry? We know Jeff's not out there."

"Hogan's afraid he is."

"How could that be?"

"If I'm reading it right, then the tracker *is* out at the end of Big Pine Road. It could mean Jeff ran off the road. Or something. Or maybe nothing, Lee. It may be perfectly all right."

I stood back, almost stunned, and Joe spoke again. "You keep an eye on Tess," he said. Then the truck dug out of our drive, throwing gravel behind it.

He left me scared to death.

Joe had stimulated my imagination with thoughts I didn't like. If the bug was working correctly Jeff was — well, lost in the woods.

Of course, Jeff really might have found the bug and tossed it into the bushes at the end of Big Pine Road. But if he hadn't done that — well, the logical conclusion was terrifying.

It would mean something had happened to Jeff.

Jeff's car might be in one of the most remote and heavily wooded parts of Warner

County. And it could be in a situation where it wasn't easily seen from the road. If it were, Tess would have spotted it.

I imagined Jeff's car in a ravine, hidden by trees and bushes. I pictured it upside down in a creek. I pictured Jeff injured, unconscious, bleeding. I stopped before I got to an even more frightening possibility.

I didn't say anything, but I realized Tess had come out of the house and was standing behind me. Her eyes were wide and frightened. I realized that she had caught the implications of Joe's rapid exit after he checked the tracking device.

When she spoke, her voice was a whisper. "Where is Joe going?"

I tried to make myself sound brisk and unafraid. "He's going to ask our pal Hogan — you know, the police chief married to my aunt — if that bug-finder app is working," I said. "You know how guys are about gadgets. They want to play with it. You'll be lucky to get either it or your cell phone back."

Tess declined dessert, even a hazelnut truffle that had somehow been misdecorated to look like a lemon chiffon goodie. TenHuis employees were allowed to bring the mistakes home free, and I frequently took advantage of that rule.

She cleared the table while I loaded the dishwasher. Then we turned on the television and stared blindly at the screen. I thought about calling Alicia, but I simply couldn't face it.

When the phone rang an hour later, we both leaped to our feet.

As I'd hoped, it was Joe.

"Ask Tess what kind of car Jeff was driving," he said.

It was a new-model Lexus, which didn't surprise me; that was the type of car Jeff's dad would think suitable for his son.

"White," I said to Joe. "She says it's white."

A beat went by.

"Joe!" My yell might have burst his eardrum. "Did you find Jeff's car?"

"I guess so."

"Is Jeff okay?"

"The car is empty, Lee. Jeff's not in it."

CHOCOLATE CHAT

In the first Chocoholic mystery, *The Chocolate Cat Caper,* Lee and Aunt Nettie hold a press conference, where Aunt Nettie begins her statement to the reporters by saying, "We don't make fudge."

That gets a laugh from the assembled members of the press. People who have been to Michigan's resorts will understand why. Fudge is everywhere.

Of course, the fudge-making center — of Michigan and maybe of the world — is Mackinac Island, in northern Michigan. This island, not quite four square miles, is in Lake Huron at the eastern end of the Straits of Mackinac, and it's drawn tourists since the late 1800s. And one of the reasons they come is fudge.

On this small island, some fifteen shops make fudge. For more than a hundred years visitors have watched as creamy chocolate is mixed, tossed, and kneaded back and forth on big marble slabs as part of informal shows. Who can resist eating some? And how can the fudge shops resist expanding into branches all across

Michigan and even as far away as New England?

Fudge is great stuff, but as Aunt Nettie says, it's not her business. TenHuis Chocolade offers "luxury chocolates in the Dutch tradition." Both are yummy. But they are very different styles of chocolate.

Chapter 5

"Hogan has called for help searching the area," Joe said. "But there's no sign of Jeff so far."

"We'll come and join the search."

Joe sighed. "I don't think that would help, Lee. The sheriff has sent deputies, and they're bringing dogs. It's pitch-black out here. We might lose you, too."

"I guess I'd better call Alicia."

"Let us look a while longer before you do that."

Aunt Nettie arrived soon after Joe's call, and she, Tess, and I worried and wept for several hours. Maybe I've had a worse time in my life, but I don't remember one. This made my divorce — and even my parents' divorce — seem like a picnic.

Not that we gave up hope. It was, of course, a good-news, bad-news situation. If Jeff wasn't in his wrecked car, then he might be okay. But the smashed-up car was —

well, it was an indication the situation could be worse than my terrible imaginings had been.

Joe and Hogan called to report when they could, usually about every half hour. The oddities of west Michigan cell phone tower placement were such that they had cell phone service, even though we didn't. They had to call on our landline.

Gradually we learned more.

When Joe had taken the tracking device to Hogan, the two of them examined it and decided that it seemed to be working. The device, they believed, was transmitting, and it was doing it from the end of Big Pine Road.

So, riding in Hogan's police chief car and using its powerful searchlight, they drove toward the end of Big Pine Road and slowly played the light over the edges of the road, looking for tire tracks or broken bushes and limbs. Near the end of the road they discovered a place where a car had run off the gravel road. Joe told me I could assure Tess that the place would have been invisible to an inexperienced person. For that matter, Joe and I had driven out there, too, and we hadn't seen it.

As soon as they knew where to look, they had easily found the white Lexus.

"Hogan said he didn't know if he should be glad or sad when he saw it was empty," Aunt Nettie said.

Tess blamed herself for the whole situation. She didn't cry hysterically; she just cried.

"Lee, I should have told you about this earlier," she said. "When we first ran into each other at the motel. But I just couldn't believe anything had happened to Jeff. I felt sure he had discovered the bug and thrown it in the bushes."

"I would have thought the same thing you did," I said. "Or I'd have believed that the device fell off. Or somehow got on another car. Or something."

We both mopped our eyes again.

"What I still don't understand," I said, "is why on earth Jeff would have gone to the end of Big Pine Road. That's the big mystery."

Aunt Nettie kept a more positive outlook. "Tess," she said, "when they find Jeff, you'll be responsible for saving his life. No one would have thought to look out there — maybe not for months — if it weren't for the bug you planted."

Tess sobbed. Even two friendly people patting her were no help. About midnight she fell asleep, sitting upright in the corner of the couch, with a sodden Kleenex in her hand. Neither Aunt Nettie nor I made a noise that might wake her. The girl was exhausted.

By twelve thirty Aunt Nettie had also fallen asleep, and I must have been dozing as well, because when the phone rang, we all jumped. In fact, the portable phone from the kitchen was in my lap, and I twitched so hard I dropped it and had to scrabble around, pulling it toward me with my crutch, before I could answer.

It was Hogan giving another report of no results. But he ended with a request.

"Can you ask Tess if Jeff usually kept his cell phone on his person?"

I had the phone on speaker, and Tess had heard him. "Yes," she said. "He usually kept it in his pants pocket."

"I'm going to try calling Jeff's phone," Hogan said. "Tess, what kind of ringtone did he have?"

She said it was the one called "blues," because "he likes everything retro."

"Good thing it isn't like frogs chirping," Hogan said. "There're already enough of those out here. We'd never ID the sound."

He hung up, and I dropped the portable phone in my lap. Then I jumped again, because I immediately heard the faint sound of the blues ringtone.

My first thought was that I was still connected with Hogan, and that I was hearing the blues ring through the line. But when I checked my phone, it was definitely turned off. Disconnected.

But the sound of the blues ringtone continued. I was quite familiar with the sound, of course. Working with thirty women, I heard every available ringtone frequently.

Now I was hearing the blues ringtone clearly. Either the source was moving toward us or the volume was increasing with each ring, as happens with many phones.

"It sounds as if that's in our house," I said.

Tess and Aunt Nettie both jumped to their feet.

"It's here!" Tess yelled. "Jeff's phone is here in this house!"

"I hear it, too!" Aunt Nettie's voice was shrill. "But where is it?"

Tess ran for the stairs. "Upstairs! It's upstairs!"

Aunt Nettie was right on her heels. The two of them thundered up the old-fashioned enclosed staircase.

"Wait for me!" I was yelling, too.

I stuck the kitchen phone in my pocket, climbed aboard my crutch, and thumped after them. Up the stairs, clump, clump, clump.

Climbing a set of narrow wooden stairs with a crutch isn't the easiest thing in the world. I gave up trying to walk and hopped. I held on to the sturdy railing Joe had installed, trailed my crutch behind me, and hopped from step to step, pulling myself up with my free arm. A lot of steps, including three narrow ones at the turn. A few times I had to use my injured foot. It hurt, but not unbearably.

I was sure glad to reach the upstairs hall. That had been carpeted, so it at least was quieter. I kept swinging along.

Our house wasn't large, and the upstairs was just half the size of the downstairs. But my ancestors had somehow managed to cram two bedrooms and a storage room into that space. Tess' room, the main guest room, was the first on the right, and I could see the light had been turned on and that Aunt Nettie and Tess were moving around in there.

When I followed them inside, the two of them were standing at the foot of the bed, staring at the ceiling. The ringing had stopped.

"Where was it coming from?" Aunt Nettie asked.

"Was it Chief Jones calling?" Tess sounded completely mystified. "Or were we hearing some other noise?"

"We'll ask him," I said.

Aunt Nettie went to the bedside extension and called Hogan's cell number.

"Hogan, dear," she said. "Call Jeff's number again, please."

She listened, then spoke again. "Just humor me, Hogan. Please. Something odd happened."

Tess, Aunt Nettie, and I stood, holding our breath. I couldn't believe we would hear the ringtone again.

But we did hear it. And when we did, all three of us whipped our heads up.

The sound was close to us. It was slightly muffled, true, but it was obviously not far away. And it was above us.

"It's coming from the attic," Aunt Nettie said.

"Where is the attic?" Tess asked, clearly mystified. "I mean, I know it's above us. But where is the opening?"

"You get into it through the closet ceiling," Aunt Nettie said. "We'll need a ladder. Or at least a stool."

"There's one in the pantry off the back hall," I said.

Tess ran for the stairs, and I joined Aunt

Nettie's call on the portable extension I still had in my pocket. She and I told Hogan what had happened.

"If Jeff has been here all the time . . . ," I said.

"Don't get your hopes up," Hogan said. "It's probably only a coincidence of some kind."

"I'd better clear the closet," I said. I hobbled to the closet and began clearing the shelf. I immediately noticed something.

"This shelf has been rearranged," I said. "I know these boxes weren't stacked like this."

"What's up there?" Aunt Nettie asked.

"Wedding gifts," I said. "Plus other stuff we'll never use but don't dare get rid of. It wasn't stacked up in the middle, though. It was a long, flat pile. I put the boxes there myself."

"Are there more things in the attic?"

"Sure. Mainly Christmas decorations."

As soon as Tess got back with the stool — actually a four-step ladder — Aunt Nettie sent her back downstairs for a flashlight. Then she opened a drawer in the bedside table and took out a flashlight that was already there.

"Lee, I don't think Tess should be the one to look up there. And I'm not tall enough.

Do you think you can get up on that ladder?"

I nodded. "After dragging myself up those stairs, I can climb anything," I said. Somehow I managed to hop up two steps of the ladder. I shoved the final boxes aside and pushed up the square wooden lid that blocked the attic entrance. Then I pulled myself up two more steps, clinging to the closet shelf and the doorframe, and raised my head and shoulders inside the attic. I slowly played the flashlight around.

I saw nothing helpful. Joe had nailed sheets of sturdy unfinished plywood to some of the rafters, creating a floor about six feet square. Cardboard boxes and plastic bins of Christmas decorations stood within arm's length of the opening. A plastic jack-o'-lantern leered at me as well.

Nothing moved. The attic had no lighting, so my flashlight was sending its beam into blackness, bouncing it off the inside of the roof.

And I heard nothing. The cell phone, if that was what we'd been hearing, had gone to voice mail, then cut off. The squirrel, or whatever our animal visitor was, was not moving. There was no sound except the echoes of truck tires and air horns more than a mile away on the interstate.

I heard feet on the stairs, and Tess said, "Here's the flashlight. Oh."

"We found a flashlight in the bedside table," Aunt Nettie said. "Lee's looking up there."

"Lee, do you see anything?" Tess' voice was fearful.

"Just some old plastic bins and cardboard boxes," I said. "Ask Hogan to call Jeff's cell again."

Hogan obeyed, and again we heard the blues ringtone, this time much more loudly. It was definitely in the attic, and close to me. But again nobody answered. And again it cut off after four rings.

The sound had come from my right. I reached over and moved the box on top to the right. Then I moved the one on the bottom, sliding it to my left.

And I saw Jeff's face.

Chapter 6

Jeff didn't speak, but he gave a soft groan.

I nearly fell off the ladder. Then I spoke. Amazingly my voice came out quietly. "Jeff! Jeff? Are you okay?"

Which proves just how stupid I can be in an emergency. Obviously Jeff wasn't okay. But he was alive.

Tess was jumping up and down at the foot of the ladder. I climbed down, and she climbed up, and somehow we didn't get tangled up. Still clutching the phone, Aunt Nettie told Hogan what had happened, and he promised an ambulance immediately.

Tess pulled herself up into the attic and began shoving boxes down through the little entrance hole. I tried to catch them and stack them on the bed.

Tess kept talking. "Oh, Jeff! Oh, Jeff, honey! It's so hot up here!"

She was right. West Michigan summers might be balmy compared to Texas, but the past couple of days had been in the mid-seventies. Because of that silly scientific rule about heat rising, plus the sun beating on the roof, that attic must have been a sweat-box.

"Don't move him!" I called. "Wait till the ambulance gets here."

"I won't, Lee! I'm just trying to clear a path to get to him."

It was more than ten minutes before the ambulance arrived. Next, Hogan and Joe came tearing up in Hogan's car, followed by sheriff's deputies in other cars. All of them were using sirens, naturally, which pretty soon meant all the neighbors from a mile around were standing in our yard, trying to figure out what was going on. There were lights and radios and all possible forms of complete chaos.

One of the EMTs stepped off the plywood sheet, and his foot went through the ceiling of the guest room. I didn't even care when I saw it dangling there.

Jeff was muttering incoherently as they loaded him into the ambulance. Hogan, Aunt Nettie, Joe, Tess, and I declared ourselves family and piled into Hogan's car to follow. The only detour was past Hogan and Aunt Nettie's house to pick up Joe's truck.

Things didn't calm down until Aunt Nettie, Joe, and I were sitting in the waiting area of the emergency room. Tess wasn't sitting with us because the doctor had allowed her to go in and stay with Jeff, and Hogan was wandering in and out.

Within a half hour Hogan reported that the doctor was encouraging about Jeff's condition. "The doc says he's mainly dehydrated, on top of having a concussion. But he doesn't think the concussion is too serious. He thinks a few hours of IVs will improve his condition. Jeff is now resting quietly. Tess was holding his hand."

I think I was a bit giddy with relief, so I laughed. "I hope someone reminds Jeff that he and Tess just see each other on campus," I said. "At least that's what he told me."

"I imagine Tess will settle that situation," Hogan said. "She seems to be a capable young woman. If it weren't for her bugging his car, we wouldn't have known anything had happened. Personally I would have just thought Jeff took off for Texas. We might never have tried to call him, never have heard the phone."

I shuddered and resolved not to dwell on that possibility. It hadn't happened that way.

I called Alicia, getting her out of bed, and promised a new report whenever one was available.

"Oh my Lord!" she said. "I'll have to figure out what time it is in Peru."

"And we'll have to start figuring out how all this happened," I said. "You might be smart just to tell Rich and Dina that Jeff had a wreck. That's really all we know so far."

I hung up and turned to Hogan. "How on earth did Jeff get into our attic?"

"Probably just climbed up. I imagine he's athletic enough to do it without a ladder." Hogan stood up. "But I need some coffee before I try to analyze when and why. Nettie? Do you want some?"

They wandered off, looking for a coffee machine, and Joe and I sat shoulder to shoulder.

I kept talking. "I see how Jeff could have a wreck and get a concussion. But how could the wreck happen thirty miles from our house and yet Jeff was found in our attic? Can you think of any simple explanation?"

"Hitchhiking?" Joe shrugged. "I guess Jeff could have gotten a ride to our house from someone."

"But what reason would he have to climb into the attic?"

"We're going to have to wait until Jeff is conscious, Lee. Then we'll just ask him."

"Will the county be handling the investigation?"

"Legally, I guess it has to be a cooperative effort. But for now the sheriff has handed it over to Hogan, since Jeff was found inside the city limits of Warner Pier."

The whole situation was totally incomprehensible. I considered what we knew, starting with Jeff's movements since he left Texas.

First point, Jeff drove from Dallas to Warner Pier, arriving yesterday.

Second point, Tess followed him, guided by the electronic tracker she hid on his car.

Third, Tess followed the bug on his car around our community. Jeff, or at least his car, went out into the wooded area east of Warner Pier. He stayed for an hour or so.

Fourth, he came back to town and drove around, ending up on Lake Shore Drive, apparently not too far from our house.

Fifth, Jeff's car sat in that area for at least an hour, according to the tracker.

Sixth, the car moved back to the area east of Warner Pier and became stationary. All this happened yesterday, the same day Jeff visited my office.

Seventh, yesterday Tess looked for Jeff at several motels, then tried to follow his car into the heavily wooded area, again using the bug as a guide. She came to the end of a dead-end road without seeing Jeff or his car.

Eight, convinced that the bug had made some sort of mistake, Tess gave up and came to our house; then Joe and Hogan were able to find the car, wrecked, in the spot where the tracker had indicated.

Nine, Jeff was not in the car.

Ten, we found him hidden in the attic of our house — twenty-five miles away.

"The whole thing is nonsense," I said.

"I agree," Joe said. "Complete nonsense. We can only hope that Jeff is able to explain it."

I whirled toward Joe. "Do you think somebody tried to hurt Jeff?"

"Maybe. The simplest answer is that Jeff was attacked somehow, maybe by someone who wanted his nice new Lexus."

I nodded. "That could happen."

Joe went on. "He managed to escape from his attacker and hide in our house. Would Jeff know how to get in without breaking a window or something like that?"

"It's possible. Even though it was almost four years ago and he didn't stay with us long, you and I still hide an extra key in the same spot where Aunt Nettie always did. I'll check to see if it's gone."

"Maybe we ought to move it from the lilac bush in any case," Joe said.

"I don't know. Maybe some other wandering friend or relative might need to get in."

We both laughed. Then Joe spoke again.

"I guess the hijacker scenario would end with the car thief driving the car out Big Pine Road and wrecking it."

"That's possible, I guess. But there's a big problem with it. Why would someone steal his car and drive all the way to the dead end of Big Pine Road? And where did he go from there?"

"I don't have an answer to that. And speculation is a waste of time. We'll have to wait and see what Jeff can tell us."

"I guess we need to keep calling to update Alicia."

"Since Jeff doesn't seem to be at the point of death, you can put off calling her again until morning." He consulted his watch. "That's only a couple of hours."

"Maybe the key to Jeff's motel room is in his clothes. He might like to have his toothbrush."

"Good idea."

We braved the ER staff to go back to the room where Jeff was being treated and beckoned to Tess. She gave us the big plastic sack that now held Jeff's clothes and the contents of his pockets. The three of us took it out to the waiting room.

"Men should carry purses," I said.

"If they have this much junk they need to," Tess said.

"By the way," Joe said. His voice was so casual that I knew he was going to ask an important question. "Does Jeff subscribe to the *Warner Pier Weekly Gazette*?"

Tess didn't look up. "No," she said, "but he checks it out online."

Joe and I exchanged a look. One mystery solved. Jeff had been keeping track of the Warner Pier news, including marriages, online. It was sort of nice to know he'd been keeping an eye on us.

I didn't say anything to Tess; we started searching Jeff's things. One of the first things we found was his billfold, and the key card for his motel room was jammed in between a discount card for Tom Thumb supermarkets and another for Walgreens.

I held up the room key. "I hereby declare Joe and I have been empowered to get Jeff's stuff out of his room."

"And to check him out of the motel," Joe added. "I'm sure they're going to keep him here a couple of days. He won't be needing a motel room."

"And when he gets out," I said, "I'm going to insist that he comes to our house. I wouldn't want anybody who's had a concussion staying on his own in a motel."

We checked in with Hogan and Aunt Nettie, then headed out. By then it was four a.m., and I expected the driveway of the Holiday Inn Express to be empty. But we parked under the overhang out front behind a small silver car. When we went inside, an oily-looking man with big eyes was checking in. Joe and I stopped at the end of the desk, prepared to wait for the only clerk behind the desk.

The desk clerk nodded to us. To my surprise it was the same man — manager or assistant manager — who had checked out Jeff's room when I came by more than eighteen hours ago. He must have a crummy schedule!

"Hello, Mrs. Woodyard," he said. "I hope Mr. Godfrey turned up."

"Yes, we found him," I said. "That's what we need to talk to you about."

The young man frowned. "I'll be with you in a moment." Then he turned back to the first man. "Could I see some identification, please?"

The waiting man was familiar looking, but I couldn't remember meeting him. I tried not to stare.

He glanced at us with those gigantic dark eyes, then looked back at the manager. "Identification?" he asked. He sounded as if he'd never heard the word.

"Yes, sir."

The man patted his pockets. "I'm afraid I left it in the car."

"It's routine," the manager said. "Our rules require a picture ID."

"Certainly. I'll just step outside and get it."

He turned toward the door, gave us another strange look with his equally strange dark eyes, and went out to the silver car.

The manager turned to us. "How can I help you?"

I smiled in what I hoped to be a friendly manner. I quickly explained that my stepson had turned up, but he'd been in a car accident and was now hospitalized. "He'll be in the hospital for several days," I said. "There's no point in saving his room. We have his room key. So we can pick up his belongings and take them to him now."

One of Joe's business cards convinced the manager we were solid citizens. He said he'd have the checkout paperwork when we came down with Jeff's stuff.

As the elevator began to move upward, I realized why the man who had been waiting at the desk had been familiar.

"Oh!" I said. "That's why I thought I knew him."

"Who?"

"That man who was before us at the desk. He looked like Peter Lorre."

"Is that an actor?"

"Right. He was in *The Maltese Falcon,* playing Joel Cairo."

"Was he the one with spats?"

"I don't remember spats, but his character is a really spiffy dresser, so that's probably right. Funny to run into someone who looks like him. Maybe he's here for the film festival."

"Lee, you've lost me completely."

"I hear that fans dress up as movie characters at these events."

"You mean Warner Pier is going to be full of Humphrey Bogarts and such?" Joe looked skeptical.

"I guess so. Anyway, it seems odd to run into a guy who looks like Peter Lorre just a few days before the film festival opens. But if he's a participant, it sort of explains it."

The elevator door opened, and we got out. I didn't bring *The Maltese Falcon* up again as we walked toward the room. In fact, I didn't bring up anything. It was four in the morning, and the motel guests wouldn't appreciate conversation. Not that we were the only people awake. I could hear television coming from a couple of the rooms we passed, and as we got near Jeff's room a scrawny little guy wearing a straw fedora came walking toward us. He didn't nod or speak. People aren't very friendly at four a.m.

We had to try the key card three times before the door to Jeff's room opened. The room was just as it had been when I visited it earlier. Jeff's shaving kit was on the bathroom counter, and his wheeled duffel bag was at the foot of one of the beds. We checked the closet and opened all the drawers, but there was nothing else. We were back in the hall in two minutes.

We had tried to be quiet, but apparently we weren't as successful as we should have been, judging by a woman who opened the door to the room across the hall as we left. She left the security chain hooked, but she sent a stabbing glare through the opening between the door and the jamb.

"I hope you're through," she said angrily.

"I hope so, too. Sorry if we disturbed you," Joe said in a low voice.

Her door fell to with a slam louder than any noise we had made.

Joe and I looked at each other and

shrugged. I whispered, "This place is full of strange people."

He whispered back. "Let's get out of it."

The silver car was gone from out front. Joe slung the duffel bag into the backseat of his truck, I tossed the kit in beside it, and we climbed into the front. As we drove away our headlights hit the small silver car, now parked near the parking lot's exit. To my surprise, the man who looked like Peter Lorre was sitting in it, talking on a cell phone.

"I guess he hasn't found his ID," I said.

"Who?"

"Never mind. I'm tired, and if Jeff isn't having a crisis, I hope I can catch a nap at the hospital."

But when we went in the emergency room door, Hogan met us with a different plan.

Chapter 7

Hogan, Aunt Nettie, and Tess were standing in the waiting room, apparently anticipating our arrival.

The huge room was almost deserted at that hour. All the kids with earaches and the grandpas with heart attacks had been moved into the inner sections of the emergency room. The only people left in the waiting room were one man with two sleeping kids in a corner, and a wimpy-looking guy in a floppy hat who was reading a magazine.

Jeff was being moved to a room, and we should all go home.

I was appalled. "Hogan! We can't all go off and leave Jeff."

"Why not? The doctors say he's not likely to wake up for a while. Maybe even a couple of days."

"But somebody may have tried to kill him! We can't leave him alone. Unprotected." I leaned in and tried to whisper. "A hospital has only limited security. We can't assume they could stop a killer if he comes back."

"We don't know that somebody tried to kill Jeff. Besides, I've asked that his room number not be given out. To anybody."

"A fat lot of good that will do! You may remember that I — me, Lee McKinney Woodyard — got around that request without any trouble when we got involved with the clown case a few months ago."

"Jeff is facing very little risk. Go home."

"No. I'll stay."

Tess broke in. "I already offered to stay, but Chief Jones said I shouldn't."

"He can't stop us! Somebody should be here."

Hogan smiled icily. "I don't think either you or Tess would be too much help against a determined killer, Lee. And I'm sure Jeff is in no danger."

"I can't stand by —"

"Lee!" This time Hogan's voice was sharp. "I know you're fond of Jeff, but he's just a spoiled rich kid who gets in trouble through his own actions. We're not wasting any more law enforcement time or money on him!"

"If it's a matter of money, Jeff's dad has plenty! Tell him you had to hire private security." I pulled out my cell phone. "I'll call and get the okay from Alicia right now."

"I'm not going to authorize it," Hogan said firmly. "Jeff is just another kid who may face a charge of reckless driving. He's not going to get special treatment."

We exchanged glares for at least thirty seconds. Then I held up Jeff's kit and spoke with what I hoped was icy calm. "I assume Jeff's razor and toothbrush are in here. May I take it to him?"

"I'll handle it."

Hogan took Jeff's kit and disappeared into the inner workings of the ER, but he was gone only a moment. When he came back, he didn't look at me. He took Aunt Nettie's arm and turned toward the hospital's exit.

"Tess?" he asked. "Are you coming with us or going with Lee and Joe?"

"My stuff's at Joe and Lee's house. I'll go there." She sounded miserable.

Joe took my hand. "Come on, Lee. You too, Tess."

His grip was firm enough that I felt that he might drag me along if I resisted. This was extremely unusual behavior for Joe. Something was going on. Why wouldn't Hogan tell me what it was?

I was still glaring and fuming, but I followed Joe out to the truck, with Tess trailing along. I could hear her snuffling unhappily.

Tess was so short and the truck was so tall that Joe had to boost her into the backseat, but we got situated in the vehicle, and then Joe climbed behind the wheel. Before he started the engine, he turned sideways to speak to us.

"Now listen, you two. Jeff's going to be okay. I'm sure Hogan has him protected. He just didn't want to talk about it in the lobby, with staff and visitors around. Right now we're all exhausted, and we're going home, and we're going to bed. I don't want to have any discussion about it. And I'd rather not have to make the trip with two women crying."

Normally Joe didn't throw his weight around like that. Again I felt sure that something was going on. But why wouldn't Hogan — or at least Joe — tell me about it?

Joe started the truck and took off. He was certainly right about one thing. We were all exhausted. He turned on the radio to a talk show, which was what he always did when he was trying to stay awake. I didn't even try. I just slept from the hospital parking lot to our house. When the truck stopped, we went inside, Tess stumbled upstairs, and I stumbled to the back hall, the shortcut to the bathroom. The washing machine was in the hall, and as I went by it, I realized I'd left the hospital's plastic bag — the bag that held Jeff's clothes — in Joe's truck. But I wasn't planning to do laundry right then, so I didn't go back out to the truck. By the time I hobbled out of the bathroom and into the bedroom, Joe had dropped his own clothes in a heap at the foot of the bed and was gently snoring.

I resisted the impulse to wake him up and quiz him about "Hogan's plan." Instead I set the alarm for eight o'clock — seven o'clock Dallas time — and fell into bed.

All I could do was have confidence in Hogan. He wasn't a fool. He knew it was likely that somebody drove Jeff's car twenty-five miles away from where Jeff was hiding.

When the alarm went off, I couldn't remember why I had set it. In a few minutes memory returned, and I called the hospital to get an update on Jeff's condition. I felt relieved when the information desk denied he was a patient. Maybe Hogan did have a plan for keeping him safe.

I called Hogan and Aunt Nettie's house — thinking Hogan might have heard how Jeff was doing — but the phone didn't even ring before it went to the answering machine. I knew Hogan had an emergency number that the police station could call, but I decided not to try to reach him that way. After all, if Jeff had a major relapse, I told myself, Hogan would call me.

I still had to call Alicia about her boss' son, even if I didn't have an up-to-date report on him.

She answered on the second ring. "What's the latest?"

"Jeff was already talking last night," I said. "He wasn't making a lot of sense, so the doctors kept him in the hospital. But they said that talking was a good sign."

"I could be there by this afternoon."

"You suit yourself. But why don't you wait a little while, and I'll try to get more information? Have you reached Dina and Rich?"

"No. This trip, they actually are off the grid. But they're due home this weekend."

"Since Jeff is no longer lost, I think you could tell them after they get home."

I'd done my phoning from the dining room, and after I hung up I saw Tess standing in the door to the living room wearing nothing but a T-shirt. Well, I hoped there was something under it.

"Any word on Jeff?" she asked.

"Not yet. Hogan is the most likely to have news, and there was no answer at his house. I'll try to call them again in a minute. Are you a coffee drinker?"

"Sure. But call Chief Jones first."

I left a message with Hogan's office, saying I urgently needed a report for Jeff's family.

"Ask Hogan please either to get me a report or tell me how to get one," I said.

I made coffee. Tess added a few garments and got the toaster out. Joe was up and took a quick shower before Hogan called back. He had talked to the nurse, he reported. Jeff was eating a light breakfast and seemed fairly lucid.

"And just where is Jeff?" I asked.

"I kind of stashed him away. To be honest, I was sort of hoping some stranger would show a little interest. Someone who might have attacked him. But it didn't happen."

"Joe assured Tess and me that was true, though we're both a bit miffed because you wouldn't trust us with his whereabouts. But Jeff might actually like to see Tess. How does she get in?"

"Ask for J. R. Ewing."

I laughed. J. R. Ewing was the villainous but fascinating lead character in the prime-time soap *Dallas* — a television hit before I was born. But he was still famous, or maybe infamous, as the ultimate colorful and flamboyant Texan. My mom loved the show and we used to watch reruns.

I couldn't imagine anyone less like Jeff Godfrey. I howled with laughter. "Texas is never gonna live that guy down."

"Just don't spread it around," Hogan said. "Don't tell even your best friend. And don't go to the hospital before this afternoon. I got dibs on first chance to talk to Jeff."

So we made our plan accordingly. Aunt Nettie, Tess, and I were to leave for the hospital at one o'clock. In the meantime I called Alicia again, and settled a minor crisis at my office by telephone. Joe went to the boat shop, and Tess primped and got a few things together for Jeff. Such as clean underwear. I snagged a robe for him out of Joe's closet.

Tess, Aunt Nettie, and I made it to the hospital by one thirty.

I've never felt sneakier than I did asking for J. R. Ewing at the hospital's front desk. But the volunteer in the pink jacket didn't turn a hair. "Mr. Ewing is in room 615," she said. "His visitors are limited. Be sure to check in at the nurses' station."

And that was all it took to get in to see Jeff. We just had to know the code.

However, I did note that Jeff was in a room right across from a waiting area, and in that waiting area was a husky blond guy who had "off-duty cop" written all over him. He was probably a member of the Holland Police Department. At least, I'd never seen him before, so he didn't come from Warner Pier.

He apparently was expecting the three of us, because he gave a little wave.

At Tess' insistence, Aunt Nettie and I went in first, just the two of us. I thought Tess was worried about seeing Jeff now that he was awake, since she had followed him to Michigan in a very sneaky fashion.

Jeff seemed quite pleased to see us. He was in his right mind, as far as I could tell, though he said his head was aching.

"Actually I ache all over," he said. "Chief Jones said he thinks I was in a wreck. So I guess hurting all over is normal. How's the car? Does it have much damage?"

Aunt Nettie and I looked at each other blankly. It was obvious that neither of us had given a thought to Jeff's car.

I spoke quickly. "I haven't seen the car, Jeff. But I'm sure your dad has good insurance. I gather that you don't remember anything about an accident."

"Not a thing. I remember being in your office, Lee. We were talking about all of us going to dinner. And that's the last thing I remember until about six this morning."

Aunt Nettie took Jeff's hand. "Don't worry about it. I'm sure nothing important happened."

"As long as I didn't kill anybody." Jeff smiled. "But Chief Jones said you found me at your house. How'd I get there?"

"Drove, I guess," I said. "We haven't figured it out exactly."

"What was I doing? Sitting on the porch waiting for you?"

"No. Not on the porch," I said. "We found you inside."

"Inside? How'd I get in?"

"I figured you must have remembered where Aunt Nettie hid her extra key. We use the same spot. Anyway, I checked this morning, and the key isn't there."

"I don't remember that." Jeff looked distressed.

"I wouldn't worry about it," I said. "Like Aunt Nettie says, either it will come back to you, or it didn't matter." I wasn't sure that was true, but it sounded good.

Aunt Nettie patted Jeff's hand again. "We're not supposed to tire you out, young man. And you have another visitor. So Lee and I will go find a cup of coffee."

She went to the door and beckoned to Tess, and then she and I left. I heard Jeff squawk as the door shut, "How did you get here?"

I was going to let her explain that.

Aunt Nettie and I took the elevator down to the basement, where there was a coffee shop. Aunt Nettie was silent as we found a table, but she was thinking so hard I could practically see the wheels turning under her wavy white hair.

As soon as we were settled and our coffee had been stirred, she leaned forward and spoke very quietly. "Hogan doesn't need my help."

"Oh?" Why was she volunteering that information?

"And I would never interfere with his investigations."

I chuckled. "I'm sure of that." Where was my sweet aunt going with this?

"But you and I could drive out Big Pine Road and look around, couldn't we?"

I gave up the struggle and began to laugh.

Aunt Nettie spoke again. "As long as we didn't get out of the car . . ."

I was still laughing when Tess got off the elevator and came to join us. She didn't even notice I was laughing.

"The nurse ran me off," she said. "But Jeff wants me to come back. If you're going home, I thought I'd pick up my car from your house, Lee. Then you won't have to worry about getting me back to Warner Pier later."

"No," I said. I gave another chuckle. "All I'll have to worry about is getting Aunt Nettie and me home from our snooping excursion."

CHAPTER 8

An hour later Aunt Nettie and I were sitting in my van at the end of Big Pine Road.

The road was lined with thick bushes and behind the bushes were trees galore. It was the sort of terrain that gives me the willies, but I was trying not to let it make me nervous.

There are two ways to look at trees — either as something to hide you from enemies, or as something that can hide enemies from you. I'm of the second opinion. I'm very suspicious of what might be behind trees. I'm more comfortable if I can see the horizon in all directions.

Aunt Nettie and I had dropped Tess off at my house to get her car so she could go back to the hospital and stay with Jeff through the evening. Then we had driven the same route Joe and I had taken the evening before, when Tess called us to say she had been following the directions of her

GPS and was completely lost. Now Aunt Nettie and I were parked at the end of the road.

Aunt Nettie was looking all around. She was a lifelong resident of Warner County, but she acted as if she'd never seen this spot before.

I gestured to my left. "You see where Jeff's car went off the road, don't you?"

Aunt Nettie nodded. "It's easy in this light, though I'm sure it was hard to see at dusk. But how could anyone drive off the road by accident in that direction? I mean, Jeff would have had to turn sideways."

"That might be logical, in a way. If Jeff came here to the end and needed to turn around — well, he might have shot off into the bushes."

"But he would be more likely to back off the road. And he would only have gone into the ditch. Not so far into the undergrowth that his car couldn't be seen."

"It *would* be a pretty freaky thing to happen."

"Someone put the car there on purpose." Aunt Nettie sounded definite.

"Have you ever been out here before?" I asked. "Seems as if Warner Pier teenagers would have staked out a spot this lonely."

"I think it's a little too far from Warner

Pier to be a lovers' lane. It does seem as if I've been out this way, but I don't remember exactly when. Why does this road end here?"

"Joe said the land beyond the fence is state land."

"Yes, but state land is usually open to the public."

"True, it often is. But look — the road doesn't end here. There's a gate."

"A gate? Where?"

"Right in front of us. A sturdy gate with a lock."

"I see it now. Also the sign that says 'no access.' And it does seem sort of familiar. Not the gate, but this area."

Neither of us wanted to get out and examine the site where Jeff's car had landed — Hogan and the sheriff had guys trained to do that — so I turned around, backing very carefully, and we drove back toward Warner Pier.

"Drive slowly," Aunt Nettie said. "I'm trying to remember why on earth I would ever have come out here. If I ever did."

"It's near the dump."

"It's at least five miles past the dump, and I rarely have any reason to go there." She chuckled. "You know your uncle Phil would never throw anything away, and Hogan got rid of his extra belongings before he and I were married."

I drove along at about thirty for a few minutes, and she suddenly gave a chirp. "Stop!"

I hit the brakes. "What do you see? It all looks the same to me."

"There's a road turning off."

"I see the place you mean, but it's hard to call that a road. Only a little gravel."

"And a gate."

"Where?"

She pointed. "The gate is just barbed wire. Look at that fence post. You can see the loop that holds the wire gate closed."

"You're right." The gate was a type I'd seen in Texas — way back in some remote pasture. It simply consisted of four strands of barbed wire — pronounced "bob war" in my home country. Heavy-duty staples attached the wire to a regular wooden fence post on the right-hand side of the opening. Strands of wire about eight feet long stretched out to the left, then were stapled to a flimsy, lightweight wooden post, one that could easily be moved. That post in turn was linked to the left side of the opening by a wire loop.

"In the past, I think, Texas ranchers used this sort of makeshift gate a lot," I said. "But now they usually build stronger ones. And most farmers and ranchers use metal posts."

"A cow could knock that down in a minute," Aunt Nettie said.

"I know, but they rarely do. I guess the barbs keep them away. But I don't know what a gate like this would be used for in Michigan orchard country. And I certainly don't know what it's doing out in the woods."

We studied the gate for perhaps a minute; then I pointed to faint tracks and a gap in the trees. "There was a real road there at some point," I said.

"Actually," Aunt Nettie said, "there still is some kind of driveway. It just doesn't get much use."

We both looked the situation over for another minute, and then we spoke in unison. "I wonder what's there."

"We could go see," Aunt Nettie said.

I chuckled. "Not until I make sure we have cell phone coverage. Monsters might be behind all those trees."

My cell phone indicated that we had service. Aunt Nettie got out of the car and lifted the wire loop to open the gate, then held the barbed wire aside while I drove the van through. We were proper country girls and knew rural etiquette, so she closed the gate behind us, even though the possibility of livestock being loose in those woods was remote.

When Aunt Nettie got back into the van, she looked excited. "Lee! I just remembered where we are! This used to be the wooden furniture place."

"The wooden furniture place?"

"That's why this area is familiar. Your uncle Phil and I came out here once when we were looking for lawn furniture." She pointed ahead. "There's the sign!"

I didn't see a sign, but following her gesture, I did see a board nailed to a tree. It might once have been a sign, true, but now it was just a board, maybe two feet long, with a bit of black paint here and there.

"They made wooden furniture here?"

"Of a sort. They made extremely rustic tables and chairs. Even some bird feeders. I don't remember ever seeing one at anybody's house."

"Location, location, location. Why on earth would anybody try to sell furniture out in the woods? I mean, this gets no traffic at all."

"I have no idea. Maybe the owners built furniture for other merchants."

"Who owned the place?"

Aunt Nettie laughed. "The next-to-the-last hippie."

"Do you mean some friend of Wildflower Hill's?" Ms. Hill lived on the site of a former commune. Aunt Nettie and I had become acquainted with her when her granddaughter briefly worked for TenHuis Chocolade.

"Originally the furniture maker may have been part of that group. I never knew the man's name. But he somehow acquired a piece of property out here, bought a chain saw, and set up business. I'm sure he's been dead for years."

We'd been inching along at five miles an hour, trying to keep out of the bushes that lined the narrow road, and now I saw a straight line ahead, about twenty feet in the air and perpendicular to the road. A roof.

"There's a building up ahead," I said.

In a moment the trees and bushes thinned out a bit, and we saw a metal barn. Beside it was a tiny log cabin. Not the designer kind of log cabin, the ones you see in magazines. No, this was a real, true log cabin. Dan'l Boone would have felt right at home in it, except his cabin might have been nicer.

"There's no sign identifying it as a business," I said. "Dare we go to the door?"

"I don't see why not," Aunt Nettie said. "We can tell them we're trying to trace a misplaced relative."

The road had simply petered out, and there was no car or truck in sight, so I parked in front of the cabin.

"Look on the porch," Aunt Nettie said.

And sure enough, two rustic wooden chairs sat there. They were similar to Adirondack chairs in shape, but they were made of wood with the bark still on. They looked uncomfortable, though they did have ragged pads in the seats.

As I said, I know rural etiquette. I tapped the horn. Aunt Nettie got out of the van and I followed her, limping toward the door of the cabin.

"May I help you?"

The voice came from behind us, and if it startled Aunt Nettie the way it startled me, she might have had a heart attack. I turned so abruptly that I stumbled over my crutch.

The person who had spoken was a young woman. She didn't look welcoming.

Her most eye-catching quality was her hair — long black ringlets all over her head. Her eyes, big, expressive, and of a brilliant sapphire blue, were almost as striking. She was slender and of medium height.

She wore the kind of jeans advertised as "skinny," and on her they deserved the name. Her black T-shirt showed a strip of midriff, and it could have been borrowed from a twelve-year-old.

Aunt Nettie regained her composure quickly. "We hope you can help us," she said. "We're trying to follow the track of a wandering relative."

"There's nobody here but me." The girl suddenly seemed embarrassed by her skimpy T-shirt. She abruptly folded her arms, up high, so that they covered her breasts.

Aunt Nettie kept trying. "He would have been in this neighborhood the day before yesterday."

"Nobody was by then."

"A young man, sandy hair. Driving a white car."

"Nope. This is a lonely spot."

"I can tell it is," Aunt Nettie said. "Is the furniture shop gone?"

"Mr. Davies died five years ago. My boyfriend owns the shop now."

"And he doesn't make furniture?"

"No. We have an online business."

"Oh! Then you don't have to worry about the lack of foot traffic."

The girl laughed sarcastically. "No. We're retail, but it's all done by computer."

"What do you handle?" It was the first time I had spoken, and my question seemed to surprise the girl. "I'm sorry if I sound nosy," I said, "but I'm active in the Warner Pier Chamber of Commerce, so I'm always looking out for a possible member."

"We're in the Blackburn area, closer to Dorinda than to Warner Pier."

"Okay. I'll let you off the hook. The Dorinda chamber can look after its own membership. But what sort of items do you handle?"

"Souvenirs. Souvenirs of all kinds. I'd show you our warehouse, but there's not much to see. It's just a bunch of boxes."

"How do you ship? I'm being nosy again, but my aunt and I operate TenHuis Chocolade. We're remodeling, and that will include a new shipping room. But we haven't even introduced ourselves."

I quickly said our names, and this forced the girl to reply with hers. She identified herself as Oshawna Bridges.

"Oshawna?" I couldn't help commenting on the unusual name. "Very pretty, and unusual."

"My parents made it up." She shrugged. "Anyway, I didn't see anybody the day before yesterday. And I was here all day."

I could feel my brow furrow. "It was my stepson. We're trying to find him."

Oshawna folded her arms again. "Sorry." She didn't offer to show us her shipping area, despite our broad hint that we'd like to see it.

But we kept trying. Aunt Nettie put on her sweetest smile. "Do you have a catalogue?"

"No. Not a hard-copy one. Everything is on our Web site."

"Do you carry Michigan items?"

"No, we don't."

"Great Lakes souvenirs?"

"No. It's mostly collectibles."

Collectibles? That was no answer at all. But she wasn't going to tell us anything — except that Jeff hadn't been there — so we had to give up. But as I opened the door of the van, I had one more question.

"I didn't even ask the name of your business," I said.

Oshawna remained stoic, but she replied, "Valk Souvenirs."

"Do you have a card?"

"No. Like I said, it's all online."

As the van moved away, Aunt Nettie spoke suddenly. "Stop, Lee! Right there, by the girl."

As I obeyed, she lowered her window and leaned out to speak to the dark-haired girl.

"Would you like a ride somewhere?" she asked.

"A ride?" The girl's voice was incredulous.

"Yes. We could take you someplace, any place you'd like to go. To a safe place."

I gasped. Aunt Nettie must have felt that this girl was in danger, maybe threatened by domestic abuse.

"Safe?" We heard the incredulous voice again, and the girl smiled. "Oh, I'm safe enough here."

"That's fine, then. But if you're ever stranded out here or should need help . . ." Aunt Nettie produced a business card from her purse and held it out the window. "We're at TenHuis Chocolade. Call on us anytime you need anything. We could come and get you. We know of places you could stay."

Aunt Nettie smiled and waved, and I turned the van around and slowly drove back down the drive. I watched, in case the girl ran after us. But she didn't.

Oshawna Bridges. I said her name three times so I would remember it. As we lost sight of the cabin, she was still standing beside the big building, arms folded.

"What made you think she's being abused?" I asked Aunt Nettie.

"She just made me uneasy, as if she was trying to hide something. I could be wrong."

"She surely has a telephone."

Aunt Nettie nodded.

"She certainly wasn't welcoming," I said. "Now I know what they mean by that old expression 'the bum's rush.' I feel as if we've been pushed off a freight train by a railroad bull."

"I guess she might just be ashamed because they're not doing much business," Aunt Nettie said.

"It's more fun to imagine she had a second boyfriend hidden in that big barn and was trying to take care of business with him before the first one came home."

"There was no car there."

"Unless the car was parked behind the barn."

"Not likely," Aunt Nettie said. "I noticed that the trees grew right up to the building."

"Something she said tickled my memory," I said, "but I'm not sure what it was."

"Then you have a better memory than I do."

By then we were back at the road, and Aunt Nettie got out to open the gate. We were outside the property and had turned back toward Warner Pier before the penny dropped on my memory. I gave a little gasp.

"What is it?" Aunt Nettie said.

"The thing I was trying to remember. It was the name Valk."

"The name of their online company? What about it?"

"Night before last, when Jeff stood us all up for dinner, I told you he had been looking for someone named Falcone or Falconi. We agreed that it would be an unusual name around here. Then — just as the waitress came up — you said, 'Maybe Valk.' What the heck did you mean by that?"

Aunt Nettie stared at me. "I don't even remember saying that, Lee."

"I'm pretty sure it happened. But what would link Valk with Falcone?"

"The bird! 'Falcone' means 'falcon' in Italian. 'Valk' means 'falcon' in Dutch."

CHOCOLATE CHAT

My friend Wade Jensen likes to tell about his aunt Ruby and her famous fudge. Aunt Ruby was known as a character, full of jokes and funny remarks that sometimes shocked the more staid family members. But her fudge was a favorite with everyone.

Aunt Ruby was generous about giving friends and relatives the recipe for her fudge. But later the recipient would always tell her, "My fudge just doesn't come out like yours, Ruby."

It wasn't until after Aunt Ruby's death that they discovered why. At a family gathering they compared fudge recipes. Every single recipe — each of them in Aunt Ruby's handwriting — was different from every other recipe.

"Apparently," Wade says, "it was a sort of final joke from Aunt Ruby."

As a child, Wade says, he often watched Aunt Ruby make the fudge. "All I can remember is that she started by melting big Hershey's bars. But not one of those fudge recipes she handed out had Hershey's bars in it."

I checked online recipe pages, and there are lots of fudge recipes that call for Hershey's bars. Which is Aunt Ruby's? No one can guess.

CHAPTER 9

I was so surprised I hit the brakes and almost went into a skid.

"Watch out!" Aunt Nettie said.

"Sorry." I took my foot off the brake and let the van slow down on its own. "You just handed me a shock."

"Why?"

"Jeff told me he had come to Warner Pier for the noir film festival. Then he asked if I knew anyone named 'Falcone.' Now I find that the 'Valk' company — which is located in the general area where his car was found — also has a linguistic link to falcon. As in *The Maltese Falcon,* the most famous noir movie of all time."

"But the girl at Valk's didn't seem to know anything about Jeff."

"She didn't seem to know anything about anything. Which could be highly suspicious in itself. I'd be more likely to believe her if she said Jeff had been there, but he left, and she didn't know where he went."

"Do you think we should tell Hogan about this?"

"Yes. Though he may just scoff. It does sound far-fetched."

"I'll call him. You drive."

Hogan wasn't available, and Aunt Nettie left a request for a callback on his voice mail. Suddenly I was frantically eager to talk to him. The link between Falcone and Valk seemed terribly important, though I didn't see exactly why.

"Call the station and see if you can find out where Hogan is," I said. "Maybe we can track him down."

Aunt Nettie picked up her cell phone, and to my relief, it rang as soon as she had it in her hand. I hoped it was Hogan calling her back. But the caller wasn't Hogan. It was Dolly Jolly, Aunt Nettie's chief assistant. I could hear her voice booming even before Aunt Nettie turned on the speakerphone.

"A friend of Jeff's is here!" Dolly hollered. "Mr. Kayro! He'd like to talk to you." Dolly was wonderful at making chocolate and at handling the ladies who made it, but she couldn't talk in a normal tone of voice. She shouted.

"We'll be there in twenty minutes," Aunt Nettie said. "Give him a truffle."

"Interesting," I said. "A friend of Jeff's. Who can it be? I should have asked for a description."

"If he was standing there, I doubt Dolly would have given you one anyway."

Aunt Nettie was right. I pictured Dolly screaming out, "He's around thirty, five foot eight, and has red hair!" and I began to giggle.

I headed toward Warner Pier as quickly as I could go. Aunt Nettie made another attempt to reach Hogan, this time trying to get the police department receptionist to tell her where he was. Aunt Nettie was sweet, and the receptionist was friendly, but she said she had no idea where he had gone. I felt even more frustrated, but I kept driving.

I made the best time I could manage getting to the shop, but the tourist traffic was heavy. Just the way we Warner Pier merchants liked it to be, I reminded myself. The curbside parking was bumper to bumper. I had to inch between two tour buses to drive into our alley, where I had a reserved parking place.

Almost panting, Aunt Nettie and I went through the back door, across the workroom, and into the TenHuis shop. And when I saw the man waiting at the front, I was terribly glad I hadn't asked Dolly to describe him.

I could just imagine her shouting, "He looks like that old-time movie star, the short one with the buggy eyes!"

Because Mr. Kayro, who had come to ask about Jeff, looked exactly like Peter Lorre.

Every fan of *The Maltese Falcon,* and of a dozen or twenty other classic movies of the 1930s, 1940s, and 1950s, would recognize Peter Lorre. He was a short man with thin, dark hair and enormous dark eyes. He often played villains, and frequently starred with Humphrey Bogart. *Arsenic and Old Lace* and *Casablanca* were two of his most famous films. He had, naturally, a major role in *The Maltese Falcon,* portraying a member of the gang that was trying to get hold of the fabled jeweled falcon.

Lorre often wore a spiffy suit and, true to his role, Kayro was wearing a vintage pinstripe and holding a wide-brimmed fedora in his hand.

The resemblance of Kayro and Lorre was remarkable.

I recognized him at once. He had been at the Holiday Inn Express at four that morning.

"Hello," he said. "Are you Mrs. Woodyard?"

"Yes. And I resemble — I mean, remember! — I remember you."

"We haven't met formally. But our paths crossed at the Holiday Inn Express."

"Of course. You were checking in, and my husband and I walked up to the desk."

He nodded and smiled.

I held out my hand for shaking. "Am I correct in thinking you're here for the film festival?"

"Exactly! I'm one of the nerds who dress up as noir characters. In the noir world I go by Noel Kayro. That's K-A-Y-R-O."

I recognized his play on the name of the Peter Lorre character in *The Maltese Falcon,* Joel Cairo. We both chuckled.

"And you know Jeff Godfrey," I said.

"Correct. I was hoping to see Jeff at the convention, but I haven't found him."

I quickly explained that Jeff had had a car accident and was hospitalized. I left out all the stuff about his climbing into the attic and disappearing for more than twenty-four hours. But I tried to end on a hopeful note.

"The doctors are saying Jeff can't have visitors now," I said, "but we're hoping he'll be better in a day or so. How can I reach you? I'll phone with an update."

Kayro gave me his cell number and expressed proper concern for Jeff, adding, "We work together as volunteers at the Texas Museum of Popular Culture."

Remembering that Kayro was a pseudonym, I had a question. "What should I call you?"

"Oh, Noel is fine. Will I see you at the party?"

"Oh, golly!" I said. "I forgot that party."

"Well, I imagine that you're eager to see the star yacht."

"Star yacht? What is that?"

"All of us noir fans are excited to get a look at the snazzy yacht that came in this afternoon."

"Oh? Is this the one owned by the main speaker for the festival?"

"Yes, Mr. Grossman." Kayro gave a rather sneaky grin. "He's quite a researcher."

Noel accepted a falcon, selecting milk chocolate. Then he tipped his fedora to me and left.

As soon as I waved good-bye, I turned to Aunt Nettie. "I thought he'd never leave. Quick! Call Hogan again."

Hogan was still not available, but the PD's receptionist had found a hint of where he was going.

"I looked at his calendar," she said. "He was going to try to make some party at the yacht club."

Aunt Nettie hung up, and we stared at each other.

"Okay," I said. "We'll go to the party."

"That sounds good. I'd hate to miss taking a look at some fancy-schmancy yacht," she said.

We told Dolly we were leaving — considering that neither of us had done any work all day, that didn't seem to surprise her too much. I called Joe and left a message telling him I was going to the party before I came home. Then we headed for the yacht club.

The Warner River Yacht Club was mainly a marina, of course, with a small building that housed an office, a minuscule clubroom that was open to the public, and an outdoor pavilion.

Yacht club members didn't have to own boats, but people didn't usually bother to join unless they wanted to keep a boat there. Joe, for instance, had his own dock at his boat shop, and if he wanted to take a boat owner client to lunch, there were plenty of options besides the yacht club. So he wasn't a member.

Because of the parking problem I assured Aunt Nettie that I could walk, despite my crutch. It was really just about a block and a half — that is, if we went out our back door, crossed the alley, and cut through an office on the street behind us. The owner was nice about letting us do that. From there we went down half a block and turned one short block toward the river. My arm got a little tired, but I managed the crutch fine.

And as soon as we rounded that final corner, I could see the "fancy-schmancy" out-of-town yacht.

It was moored out in the river, and rowboats and dinghies were going back and forth. Apparently the owner was giving tours.

For a boat lover, the yacht was well worth seeing. It was at least a forty-eight-footer, with three decks. It was shiny and white, with cantilevered companionways between decks. Apparently a bar had been set up on the upper deck, because that was where the main crowd was.

"She is a beauty," Aunt Nettie said. "I wonder what her name is."

Just at that moment, I caught a glimpse of her prow, and the name emerged into plain view.

"La Paloma."

I should have known.

Chapter 10

Any real mystery reader or film noir fan would know about *La Paloma.*

"How clever!" I said. "I wasn't expecting a yacht right out of the movie!"

Then, since Aunt Nettie had never read the book or seen the movie, I had to explain that *La Paloma* was the name of a ship in *The Maltese Falcon.*

"Interesting," she said. "I would have guessed it was named after the famous song, but the *La Paloma* yacht certainly fits right in with the festival."

"Except that the *La Paloma* in the book is a freighter. And it's not 'the *La Paloma,*' " I said. "I just reread the book, and in it Sam Spade explains why 'the *La Paloma*' is incorrect. 'La' means 'the' in Italian, so you don't need both words. 'The *La Paloma*' would mean 'the the dove.' So don't tell me that reading mysteries isn't educational!"

Aunt Nettie smiled. "Whatever they call

it, it's nice to have an elegant boat here for the festival. I wonder who found it and invited them."

"I understand the owner is an expert on Dashiell Hammett. Mary Kay found him."

"Mary Kay McCurley? Is she chair again?"

"I think Warner Pier would have to give up the film festival without her."

We joined the crowd under the party tent, and Aunt Nettie spotted a chair. She led me and my crutch to it, then immediately turned to talk with someone. She rarely left the shop, but knew everybody in Warner Pier; I hadn't figured out how she did it. I guessed it was because all the chocolate lovers in town hung out at TenHuis Chocolade, and who isn't a chocolate lover?

To my surprise, Joe showed up at my elbow. "You must have been on the way here when I called," I said.

He nodded. "I heard your message. I'm surprised you're not at the hospital."

"Tess is planning to stay there all evening, and I'll go in as soon as I leave here. But this afternoon Aunt Nettie and I spent a couple of hours trying to figure out where Jeff was before he came to our house. We found out something interesting, but I don't want to tell you about it in this crowd."

Joe nodded. "Later, then. How about a

glass of wine? White?"

"Sure. But I imagine you want to get a gander at the yacht. I don't want to hold you up."

"Do you want to take the tour?"

"I'm afraid the crutch might be a problem. Dr. Jenkins is a boater, and I don't want him to catch me walking on this ankle."

"We can probably get you into a boat and over there. You might not want to climb every companionway, but I'm sure they have a good place for you to sit. I'll find out how to get us on the list. We all have to take turns because everybody wants to see the yacht."

Joe headed for the bar, and I scanned the crowd. Still no sign of Hogan. But I did see Mary Kay, so I beckoned to her. One thing about using a crutch is that people wait on you. She came right over, gave me an air kiss, and pulled up a chair. "Hi, Lee."

"Mary Kay, how'd you line up *La Paloma*? And this speaker who's such an expert?"

Mary Kay was an important part of the Warner Pier arts crowd. Creatively she was a weaver, and her studio was full of wall hangings, scarves, and place mats. Personally she kept her hair touched up and worked out, so she was definitely buff. Financially, like many artists, Mary Kay relied on a day job to keep the bills paid.

She was assistant manager of our local branch bank, and for this party she was wearing her bank uniform: khaki slacks and a dark blue polo shirt with a logo on the pocket.

"The yacht is the perfect gimmick!" I said.

Mary Kay grinned. "I guess I should preen at the appearance of *La Paloma,* but I had nothing to do with it. The boat and its owner just showed up. He called me a couple of weeks ago, said he was a *Maltese Falcon* hobbyist, sent pictures of the yacht, and offered to take part. I checked into it and found out that he's spoken at a lot of noir conferences."

"Did you have to promise not to burn the boat up, the way they do in the book and the film?"

"No arson allowed! We don't have to be *that* authentic."

We both laughed, and I asked another question. "Mary Kay, is there a vendor named Valk signed up for the festival?"

"Valk? I don't think so."

At that point Mary Kay jumped up to glad-hand someone else. As I turned away from her, I saw Aunt Nettie. Hogan had joined her, and she was excitedly talking to him, probably describing our discovery of Valk Souvenirs. I hoped no one overheard her. Almost immediately someone interrupted her, and I could see Hogan mouth, "Later" to her.

It's hard to see what's going on at a party when you're sitting in a chair, but I kept scanning the room. Lots of the participants had gotten into the spirit of "Tough Guys and Private Eyes." There were at least a dozen fedoras, and I saw a sprinkling of double-breasted suits, vests, slinky dresses from the 1930s, and plenty of pinstripes. I saw Noel Kayro in animated conversation with someone, looking more period than ever. His wide-brimmed hat was worn tilted to one side.

Then the crowd parted, and I saw the most stunning sight of all. It appeared to be Sydney Greenstreet, in the flesh. And any noir fan knows that Sydney Greenstreet had a lot of flesh.

Greenstreet was the great character actor who portrayed Kasper Gutman, one of the main characters in the best-known film version of *The Maltese Falcon.* His large size and his suave aura were perfect for the role.

The man I saw across the room was both tall and large. He even had the thin white hair that Sydney Greenstreet had. He was dressed in 1930s yachting clothes — a blue blazer and white slacks. His shoes were white as well, and they weren't modern canvas boating shoes. They were white leather oxfords, again straight out of the 1930s.

I was sure I had never seen him before. I couldn't forget a person that distinctive. So I was surprised when he looked at me directly, and his face lit up. He waddled toward me, smiling. He was acting as if we were old pals.

I racked my brain, but I still couldn't remember ever meeting such a person. But when he arrived in front of me, it was impossible to ignore his outstretched hand.

"Mrs. Woodyard," he said in an insinuating voice. "My inspiration."

I nearly yanked my hand away. What did he mean? "Have we met?" I asked.

"Not in person. But we've spoken." He gave a little bow. "I am Abel Grossman."

A memory began to stir, but it didn't exactly bubble to the surface. I must still have looked blank, because the man spoke again.

"You kindly put me in contact with the mold maker who provided me with the wonderful souvenirs for this wonderful occasion."

He reached into an inner pocket and produced a small object hanging from a chain. He handed it to me, and I saw that it was a miniature version of the famous figurine in *The Maltese Falcon.* It was made of black plastic, and it had rhinestone eyes. It was about an inch high.

"Please accept this small token of my appreciation," he said.

I took the necklace. "Memory finally stirs! You called about having the molds made. And our chocolate mold maker wouldn't help you."

"No, but he referred me to a more suitable company. So ultimately you were responsible for the falcon molds."

I looked the little black bird over. "This is lovely."

"I appreciated your referral."

"It was no trouble. All I had to do was reach for my Rolodex." I held the small falcon up. "This is a great souvenir."

I extended it back toward him, but he shook his head. "It's for you. I plan to give them away, and I'd like you to have the first one."

"Thank you! And it won't melt the way our chocolate version will. I only wish I had a chocolate one to give you in exchange. I'll make sure that you get several tomorrow."

Joe came back then, and I introduced him to Grossman. We all chatted politely, and I asked Grossman how he had known who I was, since we had never met. Mary Kay McCurley had told him I was using a crutch, he said.

Grossman told us he was from New York State and kept his yacht on Lake Erie, not too far from Buffalo. We made polite remarks about how far he'd come for the film festival. Grossman in turn told us his crew had brought the boat through Lakes Erie and Huron, then along most of Lake Michigan to reach Warner Pier. He himself had flown here, he said.

"You are a real hobbyist," I said. *With a fortune to spend on your hobby,* I thought.

"I'm not a hobbyist at all," Grossman replied. "The black bird is my lifework."

If that remark left me looking as amazed as Joe did, my lower jaw must have been resting on my bosom. *The Maltese Falcon* book and film are works of art, true, but how could they be a "lifework"?

Joe took a guess at an explanation. "Are you a researcher?" he asked.

"Ah yes," Grossman said. I'd already noticed that he was using the somewhat affected manner of speaking that Sydney Greenstreet used in the motion picture. "I am a researcher. And a collector. Also a speaker and a writer on the topic of Hammett's great novel."

He gestured toward the river. "I hope both of you are coming out to *La Paloma* for my announcement."

"Announcement?" Joe sounded wary.

Grossman shook a finger. "Oh yes. This festival is the beginning for a new project for me. I'd like you both to be present when I announce it."

Mary Kay appeared at his elbow, and Grossman moved away.

"Well, Joe," I said, "do you think you can get me into a rowboat and onto that yacht — without a hoist? I'm not a lightweight."

"Tony is here. He'll help lift."

Tony Herrera was an old friend of Joe's, and, yes, he was strong and agile. So we put our empty wineglasses on the table and moved to the dock, where people were lining up for yacht tours. Tony joined us, and he and Joe were able to lower me into the small boat without dropping me overboard. The man at the oars assured us he and Joe could help me out at the other end of the trip. And inside of five minutes I was settled in the main lounge of *La Paloma* and had accepted a new glass of white wine from a steward in a white jacket.

The yacht was beautiful, and I wasn't surprised to see that it had 1930s decor. Its design was stark, with cantilevered stairways — boat people call them "companionways" — connecting the three deck levels. The dominant color scheme was white for draperies and furniture, with bright-colored cushions. There were a lot of chrome accents. Of course, in the film *La Paloma* is a freighter. I couldn't see that the yacht had any direct connection with *The Maltese Falcon,* but it was beautiful in its own way. Which was not my way, but it was worth seeing.

Joe toured the whole yacht, paying special attention to the mechanical aspect, the way a boat lover should. Most of the boat fanatics hovered on the "flying bridge," an extra open-air bridge that is on the highest point of the vessel. I always kidded Joe that it was there so that the captain could run the boat and join the party at the same time. Which was okay when the boat was anchored in a river, as *La Paloma* was that evening.

After thirty minutes or so, Joe came back, sat beside me, and gave an enthusiastic report on the yacht's amenities and modern technical equipment. He'd met the captain, and was obviously impressed with the man's knowledge of his craft in two senses of the word — both his nautical skills and the particular boat he was in charge of.

The man knew his job, Joe said, and also had every detail of *La Paloma*'s abilities and equipment stored in his brain. The only thing Joe had missed about him, it seemed, was his name.

"I just called him 'captain,' " he said.

By that time, I noted, most of the film festival committee was present. Mary Kay McCurley took a seat near us.

She didn't look entirely happy. "I wish I knew what's going on," she said. "Grossman says he has an announcement."

"He told us that, too, but he didn't explain."

Mary Kay shrugged. "He didn't tell me either. But I doubt it's about the film festival. And that's my big deal right at the moment."

Sure enough, in a few minutes Grossman took his place at the top of the companionway between the lower deck and the next one up. He leaned on the banister and some shrimpy guy who looked a lot like Wilmer, another of the characters in *The Maltese Falcon* film, rang a gong to attract the group's attention. About fifty people were now present, and we all looked at Grossman.

Grossman formally welcomed everyone to his yacht and assured us that the bar would continue to be open indefinitely.

"This is a wonderful occasion," he said. "A tribute to a great American motion picture and a great — perhaps the greatest — American novel."

There was a retired English professor in the room, and I saw him raise his eyebrows. *The Maltese Falcon* is certainly highly regarded, but calling it "the greatest American novel" might be going overboard. I didn't leap to my feet to argue.

Grossman continued. "And I admit," he said, "I freely admit that I am one of that small group of people who believe that Hammett's masterpiece had its own mysteries.

"Its own mysteries," he repeated in a dramatic manner, "as yet unsolved."

Mary Kay rolled her eyes like a teenager.

And Grossman spoke again. "Because of my belief, I am willing to sponsor a competition. I will offer a prize to the person who offers me a clue to the whereabouts of another statue of the Maltese Falcon. A prize of one hundred thousand dollars."

At which point Mary Kay did more than roll her eyes. She stood up and stalked to the aft railing. She looked so angry I almost thought she was going to jump over it and swim ashore.

Chapter 11

We left shortly after the big announcement, sharing the small boat with Mary Kay. Her eyes were still rolling in disbelief, and her voice showed her annoyance.

"I just can't believe Grossman has taken over our festival that way," she said. "It's a good thing he didn't get too near the rail. I might have shoved him over."

She turned to Joe. "What is the definition of a 'mountebank,' anyway?"

"A fake? A show-off? Mary Kay, I'm no expert on vocabulary, but Lee's got a dictionary over in her office."

"I can look it up on my smartphone," I said. "Why are you so upset, Mary Kay?"

"This festival is about film noir as an art form. It's not a *Maltese Falcon* convention. I don't want people going off on a treasure hunt for some nonexistent falcon."

Joe's voice grew thoughtful. "One hundred thousand dollars is big money."

"The whole thing is ridiculous! You notice he didn't say he'd buy such a statue."

"How much would it be worth?" Joe said.

Mary Kay shrugged, and I answered, "I believe one of the two known to be in existence sold several years ago for something over four million dollars."

Joe looked astonished. "You're kidding! A movie prop?"

"Right," I said. "It's just made of plaster or something. No jewels, no famous artist. If you found it in your attic, you might toss it out. But because it's associated with a famous film, it's worth millions."

At the dock Tony and Joe helped me out of the boat, and we said good-bye to Mary Kay. Her back looked stiff and huffy as she walked away.

"Poor Mary Kay," I said. "Grossman completely stole the limelight."

Joe laughed. "Are you going to see Jeff?"

It was just six o'clock, and Warner Pier restaurants didn't fill up until seven, at least in June. We decided to grab a quick sandwich at the Sidewalk Café, one of the restaurants Joe's stepfather owned, then drive on to the hospital to see Jeff.

Over dinner I told Joe about the explorations Aunt Nettie and I had made that afternoon, including the Valk-Falcone connection.

"Hogan may be able to figure out how it fits together," Joe said. "He knows the right people to talk to. But between the names and the nearness to the site of Jeff's accident, the Valk people are definitely due some questions."

"I hope Jeff has remembered everything and can give us some explanation of why the heck he climbed into our attic," I said. "That's the most peculiar part to me."

When we got to the hospital we found Jeff's room completely quiet. Jeff was sleeping, or at least dozing, and Tess was reading a paperback book she had bought in the hospital gift shop. The scene was almost domestic.

When we opened the door, she put a finger to her lips, then went outside with us.

"The doctor is saying Jeff still needs to be very quiet," she said. "He wants to keep him here for another day or two."

"Has Jeff remembered anything?" I asked.

"Not really. He says he has a vague recollection of branches flying around — I guess that was the wreck. And he remembers being frightened. He keeps saying 'I was scared' and 'There was some crazy guy.' But how this fits in with climbing into your attic . . ." She shrugged. "I don't understand it."

"Jeff must have been hiding from someone," Joe said. "Or at least he thought he was hiding from someone. That's the only explanation I can think of. We can only hope he remembers who it was, but we have to accept the fact that he may not."

We sat in Jeff's room for a while, murmuring at one another in voices we hoped wouldn't wake him. I let Tess examine the falcon Grossman had given me; then I slipped it back on. I was glad to see a burly guy in the waiting area across the hall — another off-duty cop. He looked in several times to give us a thumbs-up sign.

After about an hour Tess agreed to come home with us, and we got up to leave. As I leaned over Jeff to say good night in a motherly way, the dangling black plastic falcon bumped into his cheek.

To my surprise, he opened his eyes. But he didn't look at me. He looked at the falcon.

"I thought Tess would like it," he said.

Then he closed his eyes and apparently went to sleep again.

"Jeff!" After giving that yelp, I resisted the temptation to shake him. I might break his brain loose or something. But Joe, Tess, and

I stood out in the hall and buzzed about his words.

Jeff had obviously recognized the falcon. Did this link him to Grossman? We all walked out of the hospital shaking our heads.

We stopped at a Holland restaurant and fed Tess. Then we all headed back to Warner Pier, with Joe and me in the truck, and Tess following us. By then it was getting dark, and it was one of those cool nights west Michigan can have in June. As a Texan, I loved 'em. Texas has cool nights, too, of course. But they come in March and April.

When I looked back to make sure Tess' headlights were behind us, I saw a plastic bag in the truck's backseat.

"Oh, rats!" I said. "Jeff's dirty clothes are still here. Don't let me forget to take them into the house."

Tess' little red Ford was still following us when we drove down the sandy lane that served as our driveway. We all went to the back door.

Joe paused as he put his key in the lock. "Did you bring Jeff's clothes?"

I held up the hospital bag. "I'll get on it tonight."

True to my intention, as soon as I got inside I took the plastic bag to the laundry area located in our back hall. I opened the washing machine and began to put things in it. I tossed Jeff's underwear and socks in the machine and laid the boat shoes aside. Then I looked the polo shirt over. It was, naturally, the one Jeff had been wearing when he came by my office and when he was in the wreck. It was rather stained. I wondered idly if Hogan would want the lab guys to look it over before I washed it. I decided I'd better ask him, so I laid the shirt aside as well. Which meant the khaki pants might also need a check. I started to put them aside, but first I decided to look in the pockets.

I pulled out a handkerchief. Jeff actually had a handkerchief? He really had grown up. A key. The one to our house. Thank goodness. Plus, now we could feel sure of how Jeff got in. I found a handful of change and some mints.

The final item in the final pocket was a small paper sack. It held something lumpy.

Tess had come into the room behind me. "What's that?" she asked.

I peeked inside the sack. "All I see is tissue paper," I said.

I pulled the paper out. It was, of course, wrapped around the lumpy item. I unwrapped it, turning it over and over until I got to the core.

It was a small black object. It had a metal loop on the top and a black satin ribbon had been strung through that loop.

I held it up by the ribbon, and Tess gave a little gasp.

"Well, Tess," I said, "Jeff said he thought you'd like a falcon. I guess he got you one."

The falcon, just an inch high, appeared to be identical to the one Grossman had given me, except for its eyes. My falcon had tiny rhinestone eyes, imitating white diamonds, but the ones in this inch-high bird were green and glittered like emeralds.

Tess frowned. "You said that Mr. Grossman told you the falcon he gave you was the first he'd given anybody."

I nodded. "Maybe he was just trying to make me feel special."

"But if he was telling the truth, Lee, then how did Jeff get hold of this little guy?"

Joe joined us, and we speculated. There were, of course, a thousand possible answers.

Grossman might not have been the only person to have the idea of making a miniature version of the iconic bird. The mold company might have made a different set of bird pendants for a different customer. Or a different company or craftsman might have made one. The two birds were quite similar, but it would take an expert to say they were made from the same mold.

Finally Joe shrugged. "We'll just have to hope that Jeff remembers," he said.

"Yes," I said, trying to sound firm. "Sorry, Tess, but I'm afraid you shouldn't wear this yet. We'll put this in a safe place, in case it's evidence."

"You're right," she said. "This whole thing is crazy. I guess we shouldn't even handle it, in case there's a fingerprint."

Joe launched into a spiel he gave now and then. As a defense attorney, he knew how rarely fingerprints are actually valid evidence, and he lectured Tess on this. I'd already heard the talk, so I spent my time wrapping the little bird in its original tissue paper. I then put it back in its sack and stashed it on the mantelpiece.

"I'll call Hogan about the second bird first thing in the morning," I said. "I don't think he'd get too excited about it tonight."

"Right," Joe said. "And by morning maybe Jeff will remember where the heck he got the darn thing."

"And I'm going to bed," Tess said. "I don't know why sitting in hospitals is so tiring, but I can remember my mom saying that was true when my grandmother died. I'm exhausted."

"It'll be a good night for sleeping," I said. "I love it when we have one of these cool nights in June. I think there's an extra blanket in one of the dresser drawers in your room, Tess."

"I know it's only ten o'clock," Joe said, "but I'm hitting the sack, too. Things have been too crazy for sleep lately."

Tess headed toward the stairs, and I continued toward the downstairs bedroom. This put me close to the front door.

So when someone knocked on it, I jumped sky-high.

"Yikes!" I managed not to wet my pants.

Tess looked as startled as I felt. Her eyes got as wide as china plates. Even Joe stopped in his tracks and inhaled deeply. The three of us were completely immobilized, at least for a second or two.

Then we all laughed nervously. I turned toward the front door, since I was closest, but I didn't touch the handle. I clenched my fists instead.

Joe spoke. "Okay, ladies. You two hide under the beds, and I'll see who's at the door."

Tess and I each gave another nervous laugh. "No," I said. "I'll be brave and open it."

I hit the switch next to the front door, turning on the outside light. Then I unlocked the dead bolt and boldly threw the door open.

I was standing close enough to see that a tall man was standing on the porch. The harsh shadow thrown by the overhead light hid his face, but I could see he was holding a bundle about a foot long. He lifted his arms, shoving the bundle toward the screen door.

Then, as I watched, the man slowly tipped over backward and fell to the floor of our porch.

Joe yelled something — "Hey!" maybe — and threw the screen door open. As he rushed out he yelled over his shoulder, "Stay inside!"

I obeyed, though I moved close to the screen door. Tess closed in beside me, probably peering out under my arm.

"What's wrong with him?" I asked.

"I don't know," Joe said, "but you'd better call nine-one-one."

I hobbled into the kitchen to reach the nearest phone. With the call made, I rushed back to the door, still holding the phone, as the operator instructed.

This time I eased past Tess and went outside. I stood over Joe and repeated my question. “What’s wrong with him?” Then I saw a puddle of dark liquid oozing out from beneath the man. “Oh! That’s blood! I’ll get some towels.”

“There’s no point,” Joe said. “I think he’s stopped bleeding. I’m pretty sure he’s dead.”

CHAPTER 12

All available city, county, and state cops, plus the ambulance crew, arrived at top speed. Once again our neighbors gathered, and the phone rang like mad as people tried to figure out what the excitement was at the Woodyards' house. We were getting to be the talk of the town.

For a short while Joe was detailed to keep people from driving up our lane and ruining any tracks — not that sand makes finding helpful tracks very likely. A path was worn through the front yard as law enforcement came to the porch the long way round.

Tess and I were told to go into the living room and keep out of the way. We were joined by Joe after someone official arrived to relieve him from parking duty. A state cop stayed with us. She was sympathetic but didn't question or explain.

Then we sat. And we sat. And we sat.

I was shocked by the whole thing, but I

also began to resent the man who'd died on my front porch. Why there? Why my house? Why couldn't he have gone quietly across the road and died without disturbing us? We already had too much going on in our lives. We didn't need a stranger dropping dead on the porch.

I didn't feel grief, because I didn't even know who the man was. I was horrified, but he was a stranger. Although I'd had a good look at his body, I couldn't remember ever seeing him before.

So as we sat and sat and sat, all I could do was wonder who the heck the man was, and why he had picked our front porch for his demise.

The blood seemed to prove he'd died violently. But I had heard no shots. I hadn't even heard a car. I had seen no one running away brandishing a bloody knife or a club. Apparently the man had walked onto our front porch, knocked on the door, and dropped dead. I didn't know anything about who or why.

Even after Joe came in and sat with us, I didn't learn anything. He was quiet, apparently much more affected by the death of the stranger than I would have expected. I sat beside him and held his hand while he held mine, but neither of us talked much.

It was at least an hour and a half before Hogan came in and began to ask questions. Those questions were of the "What happened?" variety. We gave information, but we didn't get any.

At least our stories matched. I had discovered the falcon necklace in Jeff's pocket. Joe, Tess, and I had examined it and had stuck it on the mantelpiece, planning to tell Hogan about it the next morning. We had then headed for bed, even though it wasn't terribly late — between ten and eleven. There had been a knock at the front door. I had answered it. The man had fallen over backward on the porch. Kerthump. Dead.

But when Hogan's questions paused, I seized the chance to ask one of my own. "Have you found out who he was?"

Hogan and Joe both stared at me. Hogan echoed my question. "Who he was?"

"Yes. A complete stranger came up on our porch and fell over dead. Who was he? Why did he come here?"

Joe gave a little cough of amazement. "Oh. You didn't meet him, did you?"

"No! Should I have? Did you know him?"

Joe leaned forward. "I'm sorry, Lee. I thought I introduced you to him."

"Joe! Who was he?"

Hogan answered, "Jake Jacobs. He was the

captain of *La Paloma.*"

It took me some time to take that in, and I spent that time staring at Joe and Hogan incredulously.

It was Tess who spoke the words I was thinking. "Oh no!" she said. "That's too squirrelly! Just like the book!"

Then it was time for Hogan and Joe to look amazed, since neither of them had read "the book."

Tess and I explained. In one dramatic scene of *The Maltese Falcon,* the detective, Sam Spade, hears a knock at the door of his office. When he opens the door, a dead man falls in. And the man turns out to be the captain of the fictional ship *La Paloma.*

"It's freaky!" Tess said. "Someone's trying to copy the events of the book."

Joe gave a whistle of surprise. Hogan thought things over for a minute or so, as was his habit, and I resisted the impulse to tell him what to do next. Question Grossman, I wanted to say. The dead man worked for him. Grossman was an authority on *The Maltese Falcon.* Finding out what he knew was at the top of my list of important questions. Of course, I was sure it was already at the top of Hogan's as well.

When he spoke I saw that I had been right. "Alec Van Dam is rousting Grossman out for questioning right now," he said.

Alec Van Dam was a detective with the Michigan State Police. He and Hogan had worked together on several cases. The state police were charged with helping small jurisdictions — such as Warner Pier — with crime investigations. For example, their mobile crime laboratory was in our drive right at that moment, and their technicians were doing whatever lab work needed to be done.

Hogan stood up. Apparently he was through with us. He said he would leave a patrolman in the drive overnight, and a state cop would probably be there, too.

"We'll leave the outside lights on," Joe said.

"The sun will be up in an hour or so," I said. I was exhausted. It was now nearly two a.m. And the sun rises early in Michigan in June.

Tess assured us she was too tired to be nervous about sleeping upstairs with the rest of the household downstairs, and we all went to bed. Once my head was on the pillow, however, I was wide-awake.

Joe still looked upset and concerned. He was holding papers he'd brought home from his office, but he was obviously as wide-awake as I was.

So I began to quiz him. "Did you meet this Captain Jacobs for the first time tonight? At the party on the yacht?"

"Yes. He seemed to be a real expert on Great Lakes yachting, as well as on boats the size of *La Paloma* in general. I enjoyed talking to him. And I wanted to introduce him to you."

I scooted over in bed, dragging along my sprained ankle in its boot. Joe put his arm around me.

"I'm sorry about what happened to him, Joe. He must have been a nice guy."

"He was pleasant to meet at least. I only talked to him for ten or fifteen minutes. But I stood around and listened while he answered questions for other people. He was knowledgeable — just the kind of guy I'd want as a captain if I owned a yacht like Grossman's."

"Do you think he came here to see you?"

Joe used his free hand to rub his forehead. "I hope not, Lee. But I can't imagine any other reason he might have come."

"Can you think of any reason he would have wanted to see you in particular?"

"No! It's crazy. All he and I talked about was *La Paloma* — you know, her size, her equipment, the course he'd taken to bring her out from Lake Erie. There was nothing that might have brought him out here to be shot."

"Shot? Is that what happened to him?"

"I was eavesdropping when the ME made a guess at the cause of death. He thought that was it."

"Then maybe he came for help, Joe. Not to see you."

"That would be even crazier, Lee. I didn't tell him my address. I can't picture him just wandering around on Lake Shore Drive, just happening to get shot, and just happening to stumble onto the porch of one of the few people he had met since he arrived in town."

"Yes, that would be hard to believe."

I gave Joe a snuggle, and he buried his head in my neck. We lay there holding each other. I felt really glad that I was married to someone who would take it hard because a casual acquaintance was attacked, someone who worried about why things happened.

Our comforting snuggles continued. Then Joe spoke. "You sure know how to get my mind off my worries."

"You make me feel happier, too."

More snuggling went on, and Joe spoke again. "Just don't kick me with that boot."

"You know I can take it off for showers. And other important occasions. As long as I don't put weight on the foot."

Quite a while went by before we got back to the topic of Captain Jake Jacobs and why on earth he decided to die on our front porch. By then I was back in my boot, and Joe had tossed his papers on the floor.

In fact, our conversation had stopped. I think I was having dozy dreams about *The Maltese Falcon.* At least Humphrey Bogart seemed to be opening the bedroom door and handing in an odd-shaped package covered in brown paper and crisscrossed with string.

That's odd, my subconscious told my conscious self. *What can be in that package?*

My eyes flew open, and I yelped, "Joe!"

Apparently he'd been dozing off, too, because my sudden exclamation made him jump all over.

"What? What!" He sat up, apparently as startled as if he'd seen Bogart as clearly as I had.

"Joe! What was in that package?"

"Package?"

"The one Captain Jacobs was holding when he fell over. You were outside when Hogan got there. I'm sure he looked at that package. What was in it?"

Joe lay down. "I'm never going to get any sleep tonight."

"Well, thanks a lot."

"I'm not complaining. You're better than sleep any day. Or night." He pulled me over and kissed me.

"Okay, okay. But the package . . . I'm not going to get any sleep until I know what was in it."

"Lee, what package are you talking about? I don't remember seeing a package."

Chapter 13

For a moment I thought I was losing my mind. Or that it had already gone.

"You're kidding," I said. "You don't remember the package?"

"What package?"

"The one Captain Jacobs was holding when I opened the door."

"All I saw was this dark figure falling over backward."

"Joe! The package clunked."

"I don't remember hearing a clunk. More of a thud. Then his hat fell off, and I saw who it was."

I sat up in bed and held my head in my hands. "This isn't one of those times when you and Hogan decide you're not going to tell me something, is it?"

"Lee, if I knew what the heck you were talking about, I'd tell you."

"You're not pretending you didn't see the package because you want to keep it for surprise evidence sometime in the future?"

"No. I admit there have been times when Hogan asked me not to tell anyone something — and he specifically included you — but this is not one of them. I did not see a package."

I began to crawl for the foot of the bed. "Then we need to get up, get flashlights, and start searching for that package."

"At four a.m.?"

"There's a cop outside, right? He can help us."

"Lee, that whole area — the front porch, the yard, the driveway — they've all been searched by the crime scene technicians. We're not going to find anything they didn't. And I still don't understand what this package was and why you think it's missing."

"Okay, Joe. Just before Captain Jacobs came, you and Tess and I were in the living room. She was over near the door to the stairs. I was close to the front door. You were somewhere in the middle."

"I remember."

"Someone knocked on the front door."

"Right. You girls — I mean, you two attractive young women — both looked scared out of your gourds."

"We were surprised. And you looked

pretty startled yourself, big guy. None of us was expecting a caller. Then we all laughed, and you said something — I *think* you were joking — about how Tess and I could hide under the beds, and you would answer the door."

"Agreed. That's just the way I remember it."

"That made me ashamed of acting so scared about someone knocking at the door, so I flipped on the porch light and then opened the door. And there was someone standing outside."

Joe nodded. "Captain Jacobs was ducking his head, probably because the light had just come on and blinded him."

"Yes. And he was holding a package in his hands."

"I don't remember that."

"You didn't see the package?"

"I don't remember it. What did it look like?"

"It looked like a lumpy brown paper thing. Something odd-shaped and wrapped in a paper sack. The man on the porch shoved the package forward, toward me. Then he fell over backward."

"All I looked at was Captain Jacobs."

"That does you credit for your concern for your fellow man, Joe. But we've got to

find that package."
"Don't you think Hogan found it?"
"Oh!" I sat back. "Oh. He might have."
"Despite your belief that Hogan and I have no secrets from each other — we do. He certainly doesn't tell me everything he thinks, knows, or discovers."
Joe sounded a little annoyed. Which I guessed he had a right to be, since I'd roused him in the dawn's early light to ask about something he didn't even know existed.
"I'm sorry, Joe."
"You're forgiven." He waved an arm at me, and I snuggled beside him again. "But let's try to get a little bit of sleep before a new group of cops shows up and starts tromping around on the porch. Just outside our windows."
That time I had nearly dozed off when Joe asked me a question.
"In the Hammett book," he said, "when the captain falls in the door dead . . ."
"Yeah?"
"Is he holding a package?"
"Yes."
"What's in it?"
I was awake enough to get up on one elbow and make my answer dramatic. "Joe! He hands Sam Spade . . . the Maltese

Falcon!"

Joe laughed. "Go to sleep," he said.

I laughed, too. "Okay, but I'm calling Hogan no later than eight o'clock. And some of those detectives and technicians had better have found that package last night."

I didn't get to the phone by eight, but I made it by nine. Then, of course, it took quite a while for the receptionist at the police station to track Hogan down. She finally told me Hogan would be by our house as soon as possible.

At ten o'clock he knocked at the back door. When I opened it, he spoke. "I'm too old for these all-night sessions."

"Me, too. And Joe's barely up. I made a large pot of coffee."

"If that's an offer, I accept."

Neither of us spoke until we were seated in the living room holding mugs filled with wonderful black stuff.

"Now, what was this important question you had?" Hogan asked.

I outlined my recollection of the package that Captain Jacobs had held when he came to our door. "Nobody ever mentioned it," I said. "Sometime around daybreak I started to worry that it hadn't been found."

Hogan stared at me a few seconds; then he swore.

That was so unusual for him that I didn't know what to make of it. I had to ask, "Are you saying that it hasn't been found? Or that my question is too stupid to answer in plain English?"

Hogan pulled his cell phone out of his shirt pocket and made a phone call. Apparently to the lab. He identified his whereabouts, then asked, "Was a brown paper package found out here last night? Any kind of package?"

The answer was apparently negative.

While Hogan was on the phone, Joe joined us, his hair still damp from the shower, and in an undertone I explained what was going on. He poured his own coffee and stayed quiet, even when Hogan got off the phone.

"Okay, Lee," Hogan said. "I'm not doubting that you saw this package."

"I'm beginning to doubt it, Hogan. It can't have simply walked off. But after the captain just fell over that way — well, right at that moment getting help for him seemed much more important than the package."

Hogan nodded and turned to Joe. "Nobody else came out on the porch, I guess."

"I don't think that a stranger wandered over to the porch and climbed the steps," Joe said. "Of course, I was more concerned with Jacobs. I suppose somebody could have walked up behind me."

"What direction were you facing?"

The three of us went out on the porch and reenacted the scene from the previous night. Hogan took the part of Captain Jacobs, knocking on the door, then falling backward — actually, of course, he laid himself down in a leisurely manner. Joe went outside and knelt beside him, calling, "Stay inside!" to me.

I stayed inside, then hobbled into the kitchen to get to the phone.

Joe pantomimed checking for Jacobs' pulse and making other checks. "I hadn't done any of that stuff since I had lifeguard training when I was eighteen," he said.

Then I came out again and said inanely, "Oh, I'll get some towels." And Joe replied that he thought Jacobs was dead.

"That was it," Joe said. "I tried CPR until the ambulance came, but there was no response."

"Well, you told me to go back inside," I said.

"But you didn't," Joe said. "I appreciated the company. Actually I was more concerned about keeping Tess inside and — well, away from the body. I know she's a grown woman, but she seems like a little kid."

He paused, then went on. "Actually Tess did come out on the porch at one point."

"What for?" Hogan asked.

"Just natural concern and curiosity, I guess. I was still kneeling over Jacobs. All I remember is that she was standing behind me. She said something like 'Can I help?' I said no, and I told her she should go back inside. I guess she did."

We all stood there, thinking. Joe finally spoke. "I guess it's not inconceivable that someone came up behind me while I was kneeling down. That person could have taken the package."

Hogan shook his head. "That doesn't make sense, Joe. Besides the fact that you're generally an alert sort of person — well, if I had just shot someone to death, I don't think I'd have the nerve to do that."

We all thought again. This time I spoke. "We need to ask Tess about this. Actually she's not a little kid — she's just the size of one. She's a college graduate, so I guess she's at least twenty-one or twenty-two. And she's certainly extremely interested in this whole thing. I'll call her down."

"I haven't heard her moving around this morning," Joe said.

Hogan frowned a frown that was almost a glare. "I thought she'd already left for the hospital. Her car's not here."

Her car wasn't there?

"I can't believe that!" I said. I stumped my way into the dining room, where the windows had a view of our driveway. Tess' small red Ford was gone. I turned to Joe. "Hogan's right."

Joe went upstairs, yelling out her name. Then he called down the stairs, "She's not here!"

I stomped my boot in anger. "That little brat! She must have the package. And she's taken off."

CHOCOLATE CHAT

Nearly every summer I pay a visit to the Mystery Readers Book Club at the Herrick Public Library in Holland, Michigan. At one of the meetings, member Carrie Stroh mentioned that she always used a recipe for fudge that called for Velveeta cheese. It came from her mother. Intrigued, I had to try it.

VELVEETA CHEESE FUDGE

Melt together: 1 pound oleo or butter and 1 pound Velveeta.

Sift together: 1 cup cocoa and 4 pounds of powdered sugar. (That's a lot of powdered sugar. Use the biggest bowl in the kitchen.)

Mix the sifted cocoa and powdered sugar thoroughly, then add the melted butter and cheese. Add 1 tablespoon vanilla. (I added the vanilla to the melted butter and cheese first.)

Carrie says: "Stir, stir, stir until your hand cramps! Spread evenly in a buttered nine-by-thirteen-inch pan. Cool and cut into squares."

I interpreted "stir, stir, stir" as meaning

beat, as with traditional fudge. But when I tried the recipe, I discovered that mixing the cheese-butter mixture with the sugar-cocoa mixture is a Job with a capital *J*. It's extremely stiff. Beating this would be impossible. But the resulting fudge is perfectly smooth and absolutely delicious.

Chapter 14

Of course, I immediately tried to call Tess' cell phone. And of course, there was no answer.

I was so mad I considered throwing a tantrum, but Hogan simply pulled out his own cell phone. Within a few seconds he was talking to a guy he called "Bob."

"Any sign of that little bitty girl who's been hanging around up there?" Pause. "Yeah, the dark-haired one."

Another pause and a frown. "When did she leave?"

Deep sigh. "If she shows up again, keep her there." Another pause. "No, don't say anything. I'll be up there in half an hour to talk to him. I think it'll be better to see him face-to-face."

From that I gathered that Hogan had talked to the guard watching over Jeff. Tess had come to see Jeff, but had left again. And Hogan was headed up there to see if Jeff could tell him where she'd gone.

I was able to speak calmly by then. "So Tess has split."

Hogan nodded. "She got to the hospital about eight o'clock. Of course, she may be on her way back here."

"I guess the hospital is the place to start. Let me get some shoes on, and I'll head up there with you."

"Uh, Lee . . ." Joe was frowning. "Hogan might want to do his own investigation."

"Listen! For five years I watched Jeff try to lie his way out of things! I'm as good as a lie detector where that kid is concerned. And this could well be a situation when he tries to snow us all."

I folded my arms and looked at Hogan defiantly. Hogan wasn't one of these guys who rushed into things. His face was deadpan as he looked back at me. Then he grinned. "You might as well come along," he said. "I'll tell the patrolman here to hang around in case Tess comes back. But there's no telling what those two kids are up to."

So less than half an hour later Joe and I pulled into the hospital parking lot. That half hour included the time we took to finish dressing. We'd followed Hogan's car, and he hadn't cut the siren off for one moment.

It was the fastest trip I'd ever expect to

make from Warner Pier to Holland. It was also the fastest trip I ever had any desire to make anywhere. The longest stop we had was when we had to wait for the elevator in the hospital. We were definitely in J. R. Ewing's room in record time.

And Jeff was asleep.

I reminded myself that the doctors and nurses had said to let him rest. Don't push him to remember. Let him recover from his head injury at his own pace. Keep him quiet. But I sure wanted to shake him until his teeth rattled. What were he and Tess up to?

Hogan went out and came back with the nurse. "Has he been like this all morning?" he asked.

"Well, he seemed to eat a good breakfast. He took a shower. His girlfriend brought him more clean underwear."

Hogan leaned over the bed. He spoke softly. "Jeff? Jeff?"

No response.

Hogan looked at me quizzically.

Jeff's left eyelid had flickered. I knew that sign, and I joined Hogan beside the bed.

"I guess we can wait until he wakes up," I said. I winked at Hogan. "Of course, one person has died over this package already. If Tess is the next victim, I — I'll never forgive myself."

Jeff's eyes flew open. "Who died?" he said. "What's going on?"

"That," Hogan said, "is what I want to know. And I'd better learn it in the next five minutes, or you're going to be in a cell. And the beds aren't nearly as comfortable there as they are in this hospital room."

"Where's Tess?"

"That's what we're asking you, young man."

"Hogan — Chief Jones — we're not doing anything illegal. We're just trying to win that prize at the museum."

"The guy on duty at Lee and Joe's house says Tess left there about seven thirty."

I interrupted. "Hogan! Why didn't the patrolman out there stop her?"

"None of you were prisoners, Lee. He was there to keep people away from the crime scene, not to keep the residents of the house cooped up."

"But who died?" Jeff was getting pretty excited.

Hogan calmed him down and started talking.

Naturally Jeff interrupted. "The captain of *La Poloma*? The captain?" he said at one point. "The package?"

It didn't really take long for Hogan to tell

the story. "So you can see why we're worried about Tess," he said.

By then Jeff was sitting up in his bed, frowning. "I need to get out of here," he said.

"Do you remember why you're here, Jeff?"

"Everybody tells me I got hit in the head. I don't remember what happened."

Hogan nodded. "We need to know that. Until you remember, you're staying here or somewhere else quiet."

"But yesterday the doctor said that I may never remember! He said not to worry about it!"

"I'm sure that's right in a medical sense, Jeff. I doubt it would help your recovery if you could remember why on earth you broke into Lee and Joe's house and hid in their attic."

Jeff hung his head.

Hogan spoke again. "But as a law officer, I'd sure like to know."

"I wish I could tell you, Chief Jones. Believe me, I do. All I can remember is being really scared. And a lot of tree limbs thrashing around. I guess that was the car wreck. But I apparently got out of the car, and then — well, I don't know why on earth I would go to Lee and Joe's house and hide."

Hogan looked firm. "Why did Tess come

here this morning?"

Jeff hung his head and sighed again.

"Jeff, she may be in danger," I said. "We — I mean, Hogan needs to know everything you can tell him."

"But I don't know everything, Lee!"

"Did she have a package?"

"A package?"

I took Jeff's hand. "Do you have any idea where she's gone?"

"No, I don't. She refused to tell me. She said she might keep her phone turned off."

"I doubt she would have gone back to the Holiday Inn."

"No, she hasn't gone there, I'm sure."

"Does she have any friends in Michigan?"

"Not really . . ."

Had Jeff hesitated before he said that? I looked at him closely. He closed his eyes and lay back on his pillows.

Hogan and I asked a few more questions, but Jeff seemed to be out of answers. He seemed lethargic.

I finally turned to Joe. As a defense attorney he'd spent a lot of time questioning witnesses.

"What have we missed?" I asked.

He shook his head. "I can't suggest any more avenues of inquiry," he said. "Jeff's an adult. He can see how serious the risk to

Tess is."

Jeff's eyes popped open, and he sat up suddenly. "Listen, I understand! But I can't help you. Tess didn't tell me where she was going. She said she would take care of the package. And she said it was better if I didn't know anything more."

"Then why did she come here?"

"I can't tell you." He lay back.

He didn't say he didn't know. He said he couldn't tell us. Hmmm. I was surprised that Hogan didn't follow up on that one.

Joe, Hogan, and I left then. Or at least we went as far as the hall. Then we conferred.

"I guess I'll stay here," I said. "The doctor will show up sometime, and I'd like to talk to him, even if I have to act like a wicked stepmother. Joe, if the hospital dismisses Jeff — I mean, discharges him — I guess I'll have to bring him out to the house. I hope that's okay with you."

"Sure. We can't let him go to a motel, and I can't see shipping him back to Dallas."

"I'll check in with Alicia."

"And I'll head to the office for an hour or so. Then I'll be back to give you a break."

Hogan nodded. "Right. I don't think Jeff should be left alone at this point. For one thing, Tess might call him."

We split up then. I peeked in at Jeff, then

asked the nurse when the doctor was likely to make an appearance. She thought that just after lunch was likely.

Then I went to the waiting room across the hall. At that hour of the morning, it was empty except for the off-duty cop, and I told him this might be a good time to take a break. I pulled out my cell phone and punched in Alicia's number.

After I gave her a report on Jeff — leaving out Tess' escapade with the mysterious package — I took a deep breath. "Alicia, I seem to remember that Tess had been working for you."

"Right. She's real good help, Lee. Gives great telephone. Accurate with the forms. And always pleasant."

"We've lost her again."

"Drat the girl! I'm sure she thinks she's helping Jeff."

"I'm sure she does, too, but she's not. Alicia, did she have any close friends in the office?"

There was a long silence before Alicia answered, "Maybe."

"I wondered if she told anybody anything about this trip."

"Let me ask around. I'll call you back."

I paced the floor for half an hour. I tried to sit patiently in the waiting room; then I'd go across the hall to check on Jeff. Back to the waiting room. Across the hall. I nearly put a hole in the tile.

When my phone rang I jumped. "Alicia?"

"Right."

"Did you find anyone who knew anything?"

"Yes and no. Last spring we got in sort of a hole for a receptionist, and Tess found someone in her dorm who could fill in. Patricia Parker."

"Can I talk to her?"

"She's not here, Lee. She's gone for the summer."

"Darn!"

Alicia kept talking. "Lee, she's gone to *Michigan.* Summer job."

"Alicia! Wow! That's fantastic! You're a marvel. I don't suppose you have an address for her."

"Not a Michigan one, I'm afraid. Have you got a pen?"

When I heard the address, my "Wow!" turned to "Ow." It was a Dallas apartment complex near SMU.

"Dadgum!" I said. "I bet she let her apartment go for the summer. Does anybody know where she is in Michigan right now?"

"Nobody in the office does. But they think it was a job in summer theater."

"Oh?"

"She's a drama major. Her main talent is voices."

"Voices?"

"Yes, she used to do stuff for us in the break room. She can imitate anybody. Ellen DeGeneres. Tina Fey. Even guys. Her Eddie Murphy is a hoot. And, yes, ma'am, she can do me. I didn't know I was so funny."

"Thanks, Alicia. If you find out any more, let me know."

"Surely she won't be hard to find." She could tell that I was let down. "How many summer theaters are there in Michigan?"

I chuckled, though I didn't think there was much humor in my effort. "Not more than a hundred, Alicia. This is a big tourist state."

"Oh. One at every crossroads, huh?"

"Not quite, but almost."

Alicia and I said good-bye, with her repeating her pledge to keep looking for information on Patricia Parker. In turn I said I'd quiz Jeff.

Or, maybe, a miracle would happen and Tess would call one of us.

I first asked Jeff if he knew Patricia Parker and had any idea of where she was. He said he knew who she was but had no idea where she was working. Then I called Hogan and passed on the information about Patricia Parker.

"If I had a directory of Michigan theaters, I guess I could make some calls," I said. "Or maybe someone could contact the SMU drama department." I didn't feel enthusiastic about that, and I was sure I didn't sound enthusiastic either.

Hogan chuckled. "No, Lee. If you get away from the hospital, you need to concentrate on chocolate, or my name's mud with Nettie. I'll find somebody else to call all the theaters. And SMU."

I breathed a sigh of relief and went back into the waiting area. The guard had returned, so I went down to the coffee shop to get some caffeine.

It was when I reached into my purse for money to pay for the coffee that I found the little falcon with glittering rhinestone eyes. It was mine, the one Grossman had given me. Hogan had taken the one with green eyes, the one we found in Jeff's pants pocket. Yesterday Jeff had muttered something about getting one for Tess. But he hadn't been in a state to tell us where he got it.

"Now maybe Jeff can give me some answers," I said.

But he said he couldn't.

In fact, Jeff claimed he had never seen such a falcon before.

Chapter 15

I pointed out that the previous day he had recognized it, but he just shook his head.

"I'm sorry, Lee. I don't doubt I said something like that. But any memory of it is gone." He sighed and leaned back to rest his head on his pillow. He closed his eyes and looked slightly pained.

I stared narrowly at Jeff. Then I sighed more deeply than he had, sat down, and played FreeCell on my phone.

An hour crawled by. I walked to the waiting area. The off-duty cop offered me a game of gin rummy. I tried to play, but couldn't concentrate and wound up down by two hundred points. Luckily I had refused to play for money. Jeff kept napping. Joe called and said he was stuck at his office for a while. At eleven thirty Jeff's lunch tray came. I saw that he had a good appetite.

It was one of the longest mornings of my life.

The neurologist showed up at twelve twenty-two. He was youngish, with colorless hair and a thin face. He looked Jeff over and asked him if he'd ever had a head injury before.

Jeff said no. "When can I leave?" he asked.

"Tomorrow or the next day. If you keep having good nights."

I could tell Jeff wasn't happy with that answer. He also didn't seem thrilled when I told the doctor my husband and I planned to take him to our home.

"Aw, Lee, I don't have to impose on you all," Jeff said. "I can just go to a motel."

"Nope," the doctor said. "Jeff, you shouldn't stay alone for a couple of nights even after you leave the hospital. If you won't have someone with you, you're not leaving."

Jeff's face fell.

I stayed in Jeff's room while the off-duty cop went to get some lunch. I liked Jeff fine, but I want to go on record as saying that he had lousy taste in television. Game shows. Yuck.

Joe finally showed up a little after one, and as soon as the off-duty guy came back, the two of us went to the hospital cafeteria.

Finally I got to discuss things with Joe. I told him that Jeff claimed to have no memory of the miniature falcon, the same one he'd appeared to recognize the previous day.

"I guess his memory has lots of gaps in it right now," Joe said.

"I'm sure it does, Joe. But I'm also certain that Jeff is taking advantage of the situation."

"How?"

"If he doesn't want to answer a question, everything just gets vague."

Joe grinned. "You're one suspicious stepmom, Lee."

I rested my head in my hands. "Jeff and his dad taught me to recognize sneaky. I can even act sneaky."

"Hey! You're never sneaky with me."

"With you it doesn't work. You respond better to honest and open. And actually neither Jeff nor Rich was sneaky with me very often. Oh, Jeff tried it, but I was smart enough to catch on to what he was up to most of the time. So he figured out that a frontal approach worked better, and we usually got along on that basis. That's how I finally handled the kidnapping threat."

"Kidnapping? Oh. You mean your fear that Jeff would be kidnapped?"

"Yes. I couldn't get Rich to take it seriously. He'd just say, 'Aw, Lee, there're lots of guys in Dallas who are richer than me. And Jeff's not dumb.' But of course Jeff was dumb. Not unintelligent. Just inexperienced and innocent. The way a thirteen-year-old kid should be. We finally did some role-playing about how and when to be suspicious. Being careful not to tell too much about your family at school, such as bragging about your dad's money. Jeff called it 'pretending to be modest.' "

Joe laughed, and I went on. "But Jeff could manipulate his dad like a marionette. Classic behavior of the child of divorce. He played one parent against the other, and in those days Dina and Rich were still mad enough at each other for him to get away with it."

"I remember that Jeff didn't act entirely thrilled when they got back together."

"I remember that, too. I thought he was afraid that having parents who spoke to each other was going to limit his activities."

We both chuckled. Then Joe spoke. "His folks aren't here now, Lee."

"I know, but Hogan doesn't know Jeff as well as I do. He doesn't push him for answers. Or maybe he's giving Jeff lots of rope. Anyway, I think Jeff and Tess have some tricky little plan they're still not telling any of us, and I think it centers on that miniature falcon."

We both chewed on our lunch. "We can work on Jeff," Joe said, "but I'd be afraid to push him too hard."

"I agree. But maybe we could try."

So when we went back upstairs, Joe and I sat down on opposite sides of Jeff's bed. I took the side near the window, closest to Jeff, and Joe sat next to the little nightstand, a typical piece of hospital room furniture with wheels, a little drawer, and room for a bedpan underneath.

"Jeff," I said, "it might be a big help to Hogan if you could remember where that little falcon came from."

"Sorry, Lee. It's all a blank."

I pulled my own falcon out of my purse. "Grossman gave me this one, and he told me he had had them made, and that this was the first one he had given away."

"I'm sorry, Lee. I just don't remember."

"So either he was lying or someone else had similar trinkets made."

Jeff simply shook his head.

Joe, on the other side of the bed, leaned an elbow on the little bedside table. "It might be important," he said. "After all, Captain Jacobs was working for Grossman. If Grossman had given someone else a falcon — What the — !"

Joe had suddenly exclaimed and jumped in his seat. He sat up straight, frowning at Jeff.

"What's wrong?" I asked.

Still frowning, Joe pulled out the little drawer in the rolling night table. He reached inside and took out a cell phone.

"Hmmm," he said. "I thought Hogan kept your phone as evidence. This gadget just vibrated."

Jeff's eyes were wide, maybe with horror.

Then Joe punched some button on the phone and whispered into it, "Yes?"

Jeff popped up in bed, sitting erect, all signs of illness gone. "Joe! Give me that phone!"

Joe put the palm of his hand in the middle of Jeff's chest and pushed gently, holding him back against the bed.

"Cool it!" Then he spoke into the phone again. "Hello. Hello?" He raised his eyebrows, gave Jeff a long look, and tossed the phone into his lap. "Nobody there. Maybe they'll call back."

There was a long silence. Jeff pouted. Joe sat expressionless. I steamed.

It must have been a full minute before I stood up. "I'm ashamed of you, Jeff," I said.

"If something happens to Tess, it's on your head."

"Nothing's going to happen to her!"

I turned and walked out of the room. Joe followed me. We stood just outside the door.

Another two minutes went by. I heard Jeff's voice. "Hi, Tess, I guess the whole plan is blown." Pause.

"Yeah, they figured out it was you." Another pause.

"Did you find anything out?" Pause.

"Well, Lee and Joe really are worried about you, and maybe they're right." Pause.

"Tess? Tess! Damn it! Don't hang up!"

Joe and I went back into the room. Jeff waved the phone at us. "She hung up on me! I don't know where she is!"

Joe crossed his arms and gave Jeff a firm look. He appeared close to angry. I tried to mimic his expression on my side of the bed.

"Okay, Jeff," Joe said. "What was the plan?"

"Well." Jeff sighed and his gaze bounced around the room like a searchlight. But Joe and I stood our ground, both of us glaring at him.

Jeff finally spoke again. "It was the miniature falcon. You're right, Lee. I can remember having it, but I really don't remember where I got it. So Tess volunteered to go out looking for the source."

"Where was she going?" I asked.

"East of Warner Pier. She was supposed to take Big Pine Road."

Joe and I looked at each other. He laughed. "I'll go look for her, Lee. You can stay here."

"No! I can go. I don't care if there *are* trees."

"Trees?" Jeff sounded completely mystified. "So what if there are trees?"

Joe was still grinning. "Surely you know Lee is scared of trees."

Jeff shrugged. "I never knew that. But anyway, Tess isn't scared of trees. Heck, her dad worked in timber before they moved to Waco. She's been around trees all her life."

"See?" I said to Joe. "I keep telling you Texas is full of great big trees. Only they're not in the part of the state where I grew up." Then I turned to Jeff. "What did Tess say when you called her?"

"She wanted to know if I could remember any landmarks, any way she could find the place."

Joe and I exchanged looks again. "It sounds like the place you and Aunt Nettie found yesterday," he said. I nodded.

That alerted Jeff, of course. "Where? What did you find?"

I described Valk Souvenirs, but he shook his head. "I don't remember being there."

"I suspect you were, however," I said. "Now, what about the package?"

"Package?" Jeff looked a little too innocent.

"The package Captain Jacobs brought to our house last night. The package that disappeared at almost the same time Tess did."

"Oh, the package was junk," Jeff said. "Just a plastic falcon you can order from the Internet."

Joe frowned. "So why did Jacobs bring it to *our* house? That's the real question."

Using the cell phone from his bedside drawer — Jeff said it was a throwaway Tess had bought him the day before — he pulled up a Web site that sold Maltese Falcon souvenirs. And there it was. A fake Maltese falcon wrapped 1930s-style, in brown paper and packing material that looked like grass.

"Tess didn't say how she got hold of it, but I told her I hoped she didn't pay much. They're all over the Internet."

We stood over Jeff while he used the cell phone to call Tess. Her phone immediately went to the voice mail function. "She's not picking up," Jeff said.

I turned to Joe. "Maybe it would be smart to go out Big Pine Road and look for Tess."

We made sure Jeff's phone was charged. Then we headed out. As soon as we were on the road, I called Hogan to tell him what we had found out about Tess' activities. He okayed our plan to check at Valk's Souvenirs.

Then he kept talking. "Hey, we think we've found where Jeff had the wreck."

"Sure. Out at the end of Big Pine Road."

"That's where the car was. But that's not where Jeff had an accident."

"It isn't?"

"No, I think he had the accident much closer to your house. That's a much better explanation of how he got where you found him! I imagine he was shoved off the road over on Lake Shore Drive. I think he was able to get out of the car, and he ran for your house."

"That makes sense, in a weird way, Hogan. If he knew someone was after him, and he recognized the neighborhood . . ."

"Sure. He would have snuck into your house."

"And if he thought they were still after him, he would have hidden in the attic."

"I guess the bad guys finally gave up looking for him. But they took his car, drove it back to Big Pine Road, and tried to hide it by sending it off the road there. And it nearly worked."

I laughed. "One mystery solved."

Joe and I didn't drive as fast going back to Warner Pier as we had driven when we followed Hogan into Holland, but we didn't waste time. In twenty-two minutes — eight minutes short of the usual time — Joe was turning his truck onto Big Pine Road.

Almost immediately we were swallowed by trees. But I didn't complain once. I just kept looking ahead as we drove east. Of course, we were going to look for the turn into Valk Souvenirs, but I also kept an eye on the road, just in case Tess' little red Ford came toward us or was parked on the narrow shoulder.

The turning into Valk's was hard to find. I pictured Tess someplace ahead of us, driving up and down Big Pine Road, edging along slowly, looking for the entrance.

I'd guess my imaginary picture was what made me so surprised when we did meet Tess.

Because Tess wasn't looking into the woods carefully or even driving carefully. She was driving like a Texas tornado. She was wheeling down the narrow gravel road at no less than seventy miles an hour. Maybe faster.

"Joe!" I yelped his name. "I think that's

Tess coming toward us. Why is she going so fast?"

"I imagine it has something to do with the guy right behind her," he said. "It looks like he's trying to chase her down!"

Chapter 16

The red car tore toward us. Its horn was blaring a continuous blast, which grew louder as the car came nearer.

Joe slowed down and pulled far to the right, nearly off the road. The car flashed past us, the sound of its horn echoing weirdly against the trees. I got only a glimpse of the driver, but I was sure it was Tess. She was concentrating on the road and didn't look in our direction. At least she was doing something right.

Behind her by maybe a hundred yards was a huge black Jeep SUV. It looked like a dinosaur chasing a little red bug. Its grille had shiny chrome teeth — teeth so fierce and frightening that I expected it to snap the smaller car up, chew it into strips of tinsel, and spit it out on the roadside.

By then Joe had stopped the truck completely, throwing up gravel. He began to turn, swinging the truck's steering wheel in full circles, jamming the transmission into reverse, backing up a few feet, then pulling forward a few inches on the narrow road. I knew he had to be cautious. If he backed into the ditch, we could be there until a wrecker came, and we'd be no help to Tess.

As he whirled the wheel and stamped on the clutch, Joe yelled, "Call Hogan! Call the state police! Call somebody and tell them what's happening!"

I already had my phone in my hand, and I began to punch its keys. At least we were in an area with cell service. And at least we had told Hogan where we were going. I wasn't sure why that comforted me.

By the time I had alerted the authorities to the chase, Joe had turned the truck around. He floored the accelerator, and we took off after the scary black SUV.

The road was perfectly straight; I couldn't tell if Tess was even still in front of the SUV, since the larger car blocked our view of her, but I didn't see how she could fail to be.

"I'm not sure I can catch him," Joe muttered. "This diesel-burning sucker was built to haul boats, not chase panthers. He has more speed than I do."

"If you catch him, at least you have the power to kick his rear end."

"If he doesn't have a bazooka."

A chill ran down my body. Looking at the fierce black SUV, I thought it seemed only too likely that the driver of such a threatening vehicle would be armed. But we couldn't abandon Tess.

Joe drove on, aiming the big blue truck down the road like an arrow as he tried to catch up with the other two vehicles. And we did draw closer to the SUV. Tess had quit holding her horn down. Maybe she had done that only when our truck was coming toward her. But the three of us — the red Ford, the massive black SUV, and Joe's even more massive truck — kept pouring it on, roaring down a gravel road that wasn't safe even at normal speeds.

It made our terrifying trip from Warner Pier to Holland earlier that day seem like a Sunday afternoon excursion.

There wasn't a curve in that road until it reached Warner Pier. Maybe that was lucky. There were a few intersections; all we could do was pray no car came through one at the same time we did.

Joe's pickup was roaring toward the SUV. But the big black car didn't seem to know we were there. The driver must have been completely concentrated on Tess. He seemed to be ignoring the truck behind him.

And that was why Joe almost got him.

He pulled up within a few feet of the SUV, gunned his motor to its utmost, and tried to tap the black car's back bumper.

But just as he nearly managed it, the SUV suddenly swung out into the left-hand lane. If Joe had been moving at ninety miles an hour, now the SUV reached a hundred. The huge black car shot ahead, pulling up even with Tess' red Ford.

The SUV was in the ideal position to shove Tess off the road. And when her small, light car hit the thick underbrush and the giant trees, it would be torn apart. And there was nothing Joe could do to stop the SUV.

So Tess pulled out a gun and shot it.

Twenty minutes later — after cop cars from three jurisdictions had arrived — Joe was sitting sideways in the driver's seat of his truck. His elbows were on his knees, and his head was in his hands. I was standing beside him.

"Damn it, Lee," he said. "Why didn't I remember we were trying to rescue a Texas girl? Naturally Tess had a gun."

"You can't generalize about these things. I'm a Texas girl, too, and I never pack."

"Yes, but on one occasion . . ."

"So my dad's a deer hunter," I said. "So I

know which end of the barrel the bullet comes out of. So forget it. Is there anything we could have done differently if we'd known that Tess had a pistol under her front seat?"

Joe gave a short, humorless laugh. "Not a thing. But I doubt I'll forget seeing that gun come out of her window anytime soon."

"I'd just like to know where that SUV went," I said.

Because Tess had apparently not injured the driver of the SUV. She had hit the big car — all of us were sure we'd seen glass shatter — and the driver had swerved slightly. But the SUV had been traveling faster than Tess' little car. And Tess had been smart enough to hit the brakes and slow even more.

Between the gun beside it and a big blue truck behind it, the driver of the SUV apparently realized that he wasn't going to wreck the little red Ford on that trip. The SUV leaped into hyperspace and took off down the road.

Joe hadn't tried to catch it. He had swerved to keep from hitting Tess, moving into the left-hand lane — if it was possible to divide that narrow road into lanes. Tess continued to slow. I lowered my window and began to wave. Both of our vehicles pulled over to the edge of the road. Then we got out, had a big group hug, and Tess and I began to cry.

"But I didn't do anything!" she said. "Why did that guy chase me? Why?"

About then we heard the sirens, way off, but coming toward us. Michigan State Police, Warner Pier cops, and Warner County Sheriff's deputies all converged on us.

The first question, naturally, was what was the license number of the black SUV?

"I couldn't read it," I said. "I think it had been smeared with mud or something."

"Well," the state cop said in a snide voice, "it's not as if there are a lot of black SUVs around here."

He was sarcastic, but right. Our resort community was full of SUVs, and for some reason black was probably the most popular color.

Tess kept repeating her theme song. "I didn't do anything!"

Hogan was calm but firm. "Why were you out here anyway, Tess?"

"I just thought that Jeff must have been here, because of his car being found in the bushes, right up the road. Then Lee and Aunt Nettie found that business, the one that sells film memorabilia, and that obviously had something to do with Jeff. So I thought I'd take a look at the place, ask if they'd seen Jeff."

"We already did that," Hogan said. "The girl there said she hadn't seen Jeff."

"I thought I might talk her into telling the real story. I'm sure she was lying. But when I got there, nobody was around. But I'm sure Jeff must have been here!" Tess was almost tearful. "Anyway, the trip was a water haul, so I left. I had gone less than a mile when here came that big black car! First I thought he just wanted by, and I pulled over and slowed down. But he slowed, too. And I realized he was trying to shove me off the road! So I dug out!"

"Where did you get the pistol?"

"Well . . ." Tess dropped her gaze. "Well, my daddy bought it for me after that stalker threatened me my freshman year. To be honest, I almost forgot I had it. But when that big black SUV caught up with me — and I thought he was going to shove me in the ditch and I was going to be killed — after all, someone was shot at Lee and Joe's house last night! I was scared!"

Hogan nodded. "Yes, that was the time to use a pistol. But it would help if you'd let me send it to ballistics."

"What for?"

"Like you said, someone was shot and killed last night. At the house where you were staying."

Tess almost pouted. "But I had nothing to do with that. And, Chief Jones, you didn't ask me if I had a gun."

"You're quite right, young lady. I was remiss. I knew Joe and Lee don't normally keep firearms in their house, so even when a guy was found shot to death on their porch, I didn't ask them about weapons. But I should have asked you." Hogan glared at Tess, his arms folded. "Do you have any other weapons?"

"No, sir." Tess looked as innocent as a prairie flower. "I'm not going to be in trouble, am I? I mean, over shooting at the black car? All I did was try to protect myself."

"No, Tess. I've seen your concealed-carry permit. Texas and Michigan have a reciprocal agreement. You had a right to have the gun, and you had a right to use it for self-defense. Joe and Lee were witnesses, and they back up your story."

"Then can't I have my gun back?"

"Sure. As soon as we check to make sure it wasn't used to kill Captain Jacobs last night."

Tess relaxed visibly. "That's okay. As long

as I get it before I go back to Texas. My daddy took me to classes — you remember, Lee — back when that creepy guy stalked me. He would not be happy if I were to lose that pistol."

I didn't bring up the fact that the stalking episode had happened when Tess was eighteen, too young to get a concealed-carry permit. I'd let Tess and her daddy worry about that. She had one now.

"I just hope the guy in the SUV wasn't hurt," she said. And, I swear, she batted her eyelashes.

Hogan melted. Right there in front of me. "Now, now," he said. "I'm sure he's all right."

His comment made me have trouble keeping my lunch down. I'd guess I was jealous. I could never get that reaction. I'd been told I was an attractive woman, and I even had a few pageant trophies to back that up. But I was nearly six feet tall. Tess was almost a full foot shorter than I am. She could get away with batting her eyelashes.

For a moment I was so jealous I could have shot Tess with my own gun, if I'd owned one. Then the ridiculous side of the whole thing hit me, and I snickered. Hogan glared at me.

After a few more minutes Hogan told Joe

and me to take Tess to our house. "Just wait there," he said. "I'll be by to question her."

But Tess batted her eyelashes again or otherwise turned loose her little-girl charms on Hogan. "Chief Jones," she said timidly, "instead of going to Lee and Joe's, could we go back to the hospital? I need to talk to Jeff."

Hogan folded his arms and considered before he answered. "That's not a bad idea," he said. "After this maybe we could get a straight story out of you two."

He turned to Joe and me. "But don't let those two kids talk alone."

Tess gave a put-upon sigh. But she didn't say anything else.

As we left, a wrecker was hauling Tess' car away. It had paint on the back bumper and on the left side, further proof that someone had tried to shove her off the road.

Joe drove back to Holland at five miles an hour under the speed limit, I'm glad to say. That awful chase on a narrow gravel road had unnerved both of us.

As soon as Tess saw Jeff she burst into tears.

The two of them sat on the edge of the bed. Jeff put his arms around her. She cried, and he kissed her forehead, then said, "There, there," and similar helpful things.

If they were "just friends," Joe and I had a purely platonic relationship.

After a few minutes, I handed Tess a wet washcloth, easily found in a hospital room. She washed her face and blew her nose and said, "I must look awful."

Actually she looked darling. Even Joe — who had so far seemed fairly impervious to Tess' particular charms — was looking at her with sympathetic eyes.

"Okay, you two," he said, "what the heck is going on?"

"I did tell her not to go out there," Jeff answered.

Joe didn't let up. "So what's going on?" he said.

Jeff gave a big sigh. "I guess it's all my fault."

Tess nestled her head into Jeff's shoulder. "It's all my daddy's fault," she said. "If he hadn't acted like a horse's patootie, none of this would have happened."

Chapter 17

Perhaps a word of explanation is needed here. Tess' use of the word "Daddy" in referring to her father didn't necessarily indicate that she was childish or immature. In many ways she was. But that wasn't the meaning of this situation.

"Daddy" is a universal term for "father" in Texas, especially rural and small-town Texas. My own dad, who was six foot four, who got his deer every winter, and who could turn a tractor into a pile of bolts and then put it back together, always called his own father "Daddy." There's even a famous cowboy song called "That Silver-Haired Daddy of Mine." "Daddy" is just Texas lingo. Maybe comparable to the British "Mum."

If Jeff and I didn't use "Daddy" to refer to our fathers, it was because we lived in Dallas and moved in a crowd that pretended to be a little more sophisticated, so we said

"Dad." But face-to-face, I called my father "Daddy," just the way I did when I was little enough to sit on his lap.

Joe had been to Texas, and I had grown up there, so we ignored the "Daddy" part of Tess' remarks.

"If Daddy hadn't treated me like a child," Tess said, "none of this would have happened."

Jeff hugged Tess. "I'm glad you have a dad who cares about you," he said. "He was perfectly right when he reamed me out."

Jeff and Tess told the story then. It seemed they had been "just friends" for more than three years. But at the beginning of their senior year, the situation changed.

"I finally woke up and realized that my best friend was also the cutest girl on campus," Jeff said. "If she wasn't afraid of the water, she'd be perfect."

"I am not afraid of the water!" Tess said. "I just never got around to learning to swim."

"But you look great in a bikini on the beach," Jeff said. "I thought, 'She's wonderful. So why aren't you in love with her, stupid?' "

Tess smiled sweetly. "And I finally realized I liked Jeff better than I had liked any of the guys I'd dated."

By Christmas they'd begun to talk about a future together, but neither set of parents — accustomed to their long-established "just friends" status — had realized it. Then Tess took Jeff down to her parents' house for a weekend, and her dad caught them necking on the back porch.

"The first thing he said," Jeff said, "was 'How long has this been going on?' "

Jeff blurted out something like "Not long enough, sir. I hope Tess will marry me."

So Tess' daddy sat the two of them down for a serious talk. Her dad, Tess said, was named Buck and he'd worked in the building industry for a long time. Today he was a foreman, managing the crews who delivered lumber, concrete, paint, and plaster to building sites. The guys on these crews were tough, but apparently Buck was tougher. And his five kids knew how tough he was.

"I was shaking," Tess said. "My daddy can be pretty earthy. He went in the navy when he was seventeen, and when he opens his mouth — well, my mom and I just never know what's going to come out."

"He called me a few names," Jeff said. "Just in a friendly way. Like, 'I'll croak if my little girl marries some rich boy who's never worked a day in his life. But I'll croak you first.' Of course, I told him I'd worked since I was fourteen, but he shrugged that off. 'For your parents.' And of course, he was right. I worked in my mom's antiques shop. Then my dad tried to interest me in real estate, and I worked there for a few months. But I like moving furniture and packing china for Mom better than *that*!"

"Buck sounds like the kind of a guy," I said, "who thinks the word 'work' means something requiring tools."

"Also sweat," Jeff said. "Moving pretty furniture, like I do for Mom, doesn't count with Buck. Now, Tess — well, she's worked since she was sixteen, but she waited tables and such. Buck thinks that's real work."

"Your dad got me a good job in his office last summer," she said. "I paid off my car."

"Yes, but you had to work the Saturday and Sunday shifts." Jeff hugged her around the shoulders. "Alicia bragged about what good help you were."

"I didn't dare not be! I'd be back to waiting tables."

"Anyway, what Buck meant was that I'd never done anything on my own," Jeff said. "The trouble, according to Buck, was that as long as I was dependent on my dad financially, Dad could run our lives. He could tell us where to live, what kind of cars to drive, everything."

Jeff turned to me. "Man! That went straight through me. Because that's just the way things are now. I always have a good car, but I never buy one. It just appears. I have credit cards, and my dad pays the bills when they come in."

He squeezed Tess' shoulders again. "I knew I couldn't subject Tess to that kind of life. She has too much spirit. She wouldn't put up with it. She'd walk out on me, Lee, just the way you walked out on Dad!"

I shook my head, because that wasn't exactly what had happened, but Jeff kept talking. "So I went back to Dallas determined to get a real job."

Tess piped up at that point. "But Jeff needs to go to grad school. I mean, he *wants* to go to grad school. I didn't want him to get a 'real' job if it would ruin that for him."

"So Tess and I thought about a lot of things. Loans, for example."

"But I've already got twenty thousand dollars in school loans," Tess said. "I had a tuition scholarship, and Daddy has a good enough job. He and my mom have helped me a lot, but — well, there *are* five of us."

"So borrowing seemed like the last resort," Jeff said. "I talked to the financial aid office at UT, but they were already offering me a slot as a graduate assistant, and they muttered a lot about 'need.' Which meant they thought my dad should pick up the tab."

"Of course, I could get a job," Tess said.

"But it would be part-time, or you'd give up grad school, too."

"We could take turns!"

Jeff turned back to Joe and me. "It's complicated. And it began to look as if I could either give up grad school or give up getting married."

Or he could give up Buck's respect. I could see that Jeff needed that. Buck must be quite a guy.

"I realized that I couldn't even buy Tess an engagement ring," Jeff said.

Then, during his internship at the Texas Museum of Popular Culture, Jeff picked up a hint at how to make some money.

"The curator asked me to check out the availability of something online, and while I was doing that, I got the idea of looking at film memorabilia. And, Lee, I found out those movie posters you gave me are really valuable!"

He smiled at me winningly. "I hope you're not going to be mad. I sold them!"

"That's okay." I laughed at the memory. Back when Jeff and I were stuck with each other's company and used to spend our weekends watching old private eye movies, he asked me to take him to visit a movie memorabilia shop. He was fascinated with it. So on his next birthday, I bought him two of the posters he had liked.

"Of course," Jeff said, "over the years I had acquired a bunch more of them. By selling them I made enough money to buy Tess a *small* diamond — but . . ."

Tess was shaking her head like mad. "But I said no! I told Jeff he'd be smarter to spend the money on more posters and stuff. Maybe he'd wind up with a real business."

Jeff shrugged. "So since February I've been buying and selling noir memorabilia online. I've also gone to several movie festivals and picked up more items. And I've done all right."

"Why didn't you tell us this?" I asked.

Jeff dropped his head. "I was planning to tell you all the night I asked everybody to go to dinner. But while I was in school, in a way it wasn't strictly ethical. See, museum employees aren't supposed to deal in items similar to ones their museums hold in collections. But I couldn't quit the museum until the semester was over because I was getting class credit I needed to graduate. I explained what I was doing to the curator, and he said it was okay because I was working with the music collection, not films. But

I still felt uneasy."

Joe cleared his throat. "Let's forget the ethics of the museum business for a moment. What brought you to Warner Pier?"

"It started because I bought some *Maltese Falcon* posters online. Not originals, just reproductions. But I thought maybe I could sell them at a Texas noir festival. I got them from a company called Falcone Memorabilia. They mailed them to me. Very routine."

"Falcone?" Joe asked. "That's the name you mentioned when you first arrived in Warner Pier. Where is this company?"

"That's a good question. I didn't worry about where it was when I ordered online, but when I got the package of posters, the postmark was Grand Rapids. You know, one of those postmarks that covers a large area. And the address on the package they sent was not readable.

"The next thing I know, I get this e-mail. The guy says he's with Falcone Memorabilia, and he offers me *Maltese Falcon* pendants. Plastic, with green rhinestone eyes."

"Like the one we found in your pocket?" I asked.

"I guess so. I remember him e-mailing me about them, but I do not remember buying them! I know the price was reasonable, so I must have ordered them to resell at the film festival — and to give to Tess. Anyway, after that the tone of the e-mails kind of changed. The guy claimed he had some special falcon items, and he asked if I'd be interested in them."

Jeff looked worried. "He sounded weird. I almost expected him to say he had 'feelthy pictures.'

"I sloughed the first message off, but next he told me that the plastic pendants were replicas of a more valuable one, one that had been made especially for Mary Astor. And he could get the original. Then I began to get interested."

Joe looked blank, and I remembered he had little interest in film noir.

"Mary Astor was the female star of *The Maltese Falcon,* Joe," I said.

Joe nodded, and Jeff went on. "The guy from Falcone Memorabilia said some boyfriend had the little falcon made for her, enamel, with diamond eyes. And Falcone had it for sale. I asked how he got hold of it, and he e-mailed something about 'its provenance is a little cloudy.' So I let it drop."

"A lot of dealers aren't so picky," Joe said.

"A lot of dealers are stupid, too. I might

not be any more honest than the other guys, but an enamel pendant isn't worth a lot, even with diamonds. The only thing that would make it valuable would be the connection with Mary Astor. And if you can't *prove* that, it would be worth very little. Basically just the value of the diamonds. Heck, if it had a perfect provenance, it still wouldn't be worth a lot."

"Why not?" Joe asked.

"First, it wasn't in the film. Second, Mary Astor wasn't as big a star as Bogart became. So I didn't bite. But they e-mailed me a few more times hinting at even more valuable items. Then I ran into Grossman."

"Grossman? You know that guy?"

"Tess' dad would say we've howdied, but we ain't shook. Grossman visited our museum, and he got a guided tour from the director. He has a pretty big reputation in the noir world. As he came by where I was working, he was talking about this grant he was going to give the museum, for the five-thousand-dollar prize. Then he assured the director that he'd done a lot of research — actually I think he hires a researcher — and he could prove that a third Maltese Falcon prop existed. I work with this guy named Hal Hale, another volunteer, who's also a noir fan, and we could hardly wait for

Grossman to leave so we could laugh."

"Why?" Joe asked.

"Because we were both sure there is no third Maltese Falcon. Grossman claimed to be such a big authority and he didn't know crap."

Joe was looking mystified again. I spoke. "Jeff, you've lost Joe again. Better explain."

Jeff laughed. "These newbies! You know what the falcon is, don't you?"

"Sure. Lee made me watch the movie. It's the statue the villains are after in *The Maltese Falcon.*"

"Right. There were two falcons made as props in the film. Only two."

"Not three, like Grossman claims?"

"Two. That's really well established. Both of them are in the hands of private collectors." Jeff leaned over and dropped his voice. "The last time one sold, at auction, it brought more than four million dollars."

Joe nodded. "That's what Mary Kay told us. So if a third falcon was discovered . . ."

"It would be worth a boatload of money. But it would need really impressive provenance to prove its authenticity. And it would be auctioned by Sotheby's, not sold by e-mail by some company in rural Michigan that nobody ever heard of.

"I really wanted to win the contest for

five thousand dollars though, so I decided maybe I ought to visit the Falcone place personally and get a look at everything they had. But I had no address for them, just a zip. And that zip code takes in a lot of Michigan."

Joe looked a little more interested. "I assumed you had used a credit card to buy from them."

"Yeah. But the information on my bill was vague."

"Then how'd you find the place?"

"I'm not sure I did! I don't remember going there. But I tried to find it. I called Visa and complained that someone had charged something on my bill that I hadn't ordered. The Visa lady told me where the charge had been handled. It was a post box number in Dorinda, Michigan. So that way I got the name of the town. Then I told Visa that I just hadn't recognized the charge and apologized for bothering them."

"But knowing a town doesn't tell you where to find them."

"Right." Jeff grinned. "So the first day I got here, the morning of the day I went by to see Lee, I went over to the Dorinda Post Office and asked the postmaster where Falcone Memorabilia was. He told me he didn't know, since the box holders picked up their mail at the office. Then he grinned at me and said, 'Information central for this town is the Dorinda Donut Shop. Go out the door and turn left.' "

Joe looked at me, and we both laughed. "There are no secrets in a small town," I said. "Did the doughnut shop tell you?"

"The cashier didn't know, but one of the customers did. He said it was 'the old Valk place.' "

CHOCOLATE CHAT

The most famous name in American chocolate is, of course, Hershey's. Here's their recipe for fudge.

HERSHEY'S OLD-FASHIONED RICH COCOA FUDGE

3 cups sugar
2/3 cup cocoa
1/8 teaspoon salt
1 1/2 cups whole milk
1/4 cup real butter
1 teaspoon vanilla extract

Line 8- or 9-inch square pan with foil. Butter foil. In large, heavy saucepan, stir together sugar, cocoa, and salt. Stir in milk, using wooden spoon. Cook over medium heat, stirring constantly, until mixture comes to full rolling boil. Boil without stirring to 234 degrees F on candy thermometer. This can take 20 to 30 minutes. Remove from heat. Add butter and vanilla. DO NOT STIR. Cool at room temperature to 110 degrees F, or lukewarm. (This may take two to two and a half hours.) Beat with wooden spoon until fudge thickens and loses some gloss. (This much beating is work. Find a partner.) When it begins to look more like frosting than like syrup, pour into prepared pan. Cool before cutting into squares. Best made with whole milk and real butter.

CHAPTER 18

Jeff spoke again. "I honestly don't remember finding Falcone's. All of you are sure I went to this place out in the boonies, but it's a mystery to me."

I ignored that and asked the question we were all thinking about. "Okay. In that final e-mail, just what did the Falcone man tell you?"

"He claimed that a third falcon does exist, just not in the form we all expect. It would be an incredible find, if it's true. But I have my doubts."

"In this situation," I said, "you're probably wise to be cautious. This certainly could be a setup for a con job preying on noir fans."

Then I felt embarrassed. After all, Jeff was a big-time noir fan himself. Would he take offense?

But apparently my remark hadn't upset Jeff. "You're totally right, Lee," he said.

"Someone like Grossman could easily simply be a con man."

"What makes you suspicious of a prominent collector like Grossman when it comes to a movie prop?" Joe asked.

"The Maltese Falcon props are so well-known — they're documented upside down and backward. It's just not possible that a third falcon *of the same* type exists. But when Grossman talks about another falcon, he could mean something different. I'm sure I wouldn't be able to buy it, but I'd sure like to see it."

"I heard what Grossman said about the contest he was sponsoring," I said. "He didn't offer a hundred thousand for the statuette. He offered the money for a clue to where it could be found."

Jeff grinned. "Oh. If that's the case, I might win the money. All I have to do is find out if Falcone has a real falcon and then let Grossman know."

I crossed my eyes. "But you said it didn't exist."

"Something *like it* might exist." Jeff sat forward and dropped his voice. "If a movie prop man was given the job of creating a falcon, wouldn't he test several designs? See which one he liked? And see which one the director liked?"

Joe nodded slowly. "So you mean the falcon Grossman is talking about might not look like — I guess we could call it the 'Bogart falcon'?"

"Exactly! If you look at the first edition of the book, for example, the falcon on the cover is nothing like the movie falcon. It's slimmer, more art deco. In fact, there's long been a belief that Hammett got the idea to use the falcon as the MacGuffin from a real jeweled falcon owned by a British nobleman."

Joe shook his head. "Okay. You lost me. 'Use the falcon as the MacGuffin'? What does that mean?"

Jeff looked pained, so I answered Joe's question. "Jeff taught me that term when he was fourteen. Let's see if I remember. A MacGuffin is a plot device. It's the object that everybody in the movie is after. It's the thing that makes the plot move along."

That made Jeff look a little happier. "Right, Lee! And it can be anything."

Joe looked even more confused.

"Joe," Jeff said, "what's your favorite movie?"

"I don't have one."

"Try *The Maltese Falcon* itself," I said to Jeff. "Since Joe and I watched it recently."

"Okay. In *The Maltese Falcon* what are all

the characters trying to get hold of?"

"A statue of a bird."

"Right. But what if it had been a statue of something else? A saint, maybe. Or an elephant. Or a Roman Venus. The movie plot would still work."

"I see," Joe said. "Because the movie isn't really about the falcon statue. It's about the characters and the choices they have to make as they try to get hold of it. Right?"

"Exactly! And it's especially about Sam Spade and the choices he makes. That's what makes it such a great film! The statue is just the device Hammett picked to motivate the characters."

"And movie fans call that the MacGuffin?"

"Moviemakers and movie fans. Sometimes writers. Everybody at this film festival would know what a MacGuffin is. And Hammett could have used a million different things. A fabulous diamond. A prize racehorse. The heir to a throne. A twelfth-century map proving that Erik the Red discovered America."

"But Hammett picked a falcon."

"You got it! And one of the guesses as to why he chose a falcon is that he was inspired by this actual jeweled bird, very historic."

"I see."

Jeff gestured vigorously. "So, if you were a movie prop designer, and you had to make a statue of an ancient jeweled bird for a film, how would you start?"

"Well, I'm a lawyer. We start by researching. I'd try to find out what actual bird statues of the appropriate time period looked like. Then I'd probably make a model. I'd either draw one or make one out of clay or some other inexpensive material. I'd get an okay from the producer before I made the real one."

"Exactly! And I think that's what the Falcone guy has. A model of a proposed falcon. Probably one the producer turned down."

"That could be."

Jeff went on, but his voice sounded a bit weaker. "Someplace I've got a picture of the famous jeweled statue . . . It's in a well-known collection of art in England. The falcon in it is much more lifelike than the Bogart falcon, which is stylized. And it's definitely covered with jewels."

"Did the Falcone guy describe his falcon?"

Jeff sat silently, rubbing his forehead and frowning. "I can't recall exactly what he said."

Suddenly we all remembered something more important than a jeweled falcon. Jeff was recovering from a concussion.

Tess jumped to her feet. "Jeff! Honey! You lie down."

"Yes, Jeff. We've tired you out," I said.

In five minutes we had Jeff tucked in bed, had consulted the nurse — who wasn't real happy with us — and had dimmed the lights.

"I guess I *am* getting tired," Jeff said. "But I wish I could remember just how he described the statue. I need my computer."

This time I didn't feel as if he was using his injury to keep from talking to me.

Tess, Joe, and I settled in the empty waiting area across the hall. Tess and I grabbed a couch, and Joe moved to a corner and pulled out his phone, saying he needed to check in with his office.

He had barely put his phone to his ear when Tess turned to me. She spoke quietly. "Lee, I'd like to ask you a personal question."

What was coming? "Sure, Tess."

"Is there something wrong with Jeff's daddy?"

"Not that I know of. What brought that on?"

"I mean . . ." She wiggled uncomfortably. "I know it's none of my business, Lee, but Jeff said something about 'why you walked out on' him."

"Oh. Well, if you're going to join the family, I guess you deserve to know the family secrets. Rich didn't beat me or anything, Tess. We just weren't happy together. We were both seeing counselors more than we were seeing each other."

She didn't look satisfied. And maybe she did deserve a better answer. The problem was, I wasn't sure I could give her one.

"Let me think a minute," I said. And I took a full minute to try to analyze what I wanted to say.

Finally I spoke. "As they say, Tess, it was as much my fault as Rich's. See, my parents were always hard up, and they were always arguing about money. Then they divorced, and I thought it was because of their money problems. So when I met Jeff's dad, part of me may have thought, 'Well, at least we won't have to worry about money.' But I also fell for Rich big-time! I would never want you to think I married him for his money. I was crazy about him. But after we were married — well, it's the way your dad figured it — Rich saw money as control. He wanted to make all the decisions, and not just the financial decisions. He wasn't mean about it; he just thought he knew best. If I tried to talk to him, then he saw that he'd hurt my feelings. That made him feel bad, and he wanted to apologize. But instead of trying to understand my viewpoint, he'd buy me a new car or a piece of jewelry."

Tess made a sympathetic noise. "And that wasn't what you wanted."

"No. I didn't want *things.* I wanted some — respect, I guess. He wanted gratitude. And he wanted to show me off as if I were a possession. Neither of us was getting what we wanted out of the marriage. It got to the point we were at odds all the time. And I don't want to live like that. So I left."

"Jeff told me you refused any kind of financial settlement. Why?"

"I felt that money had been at the center of our problems, and I wanted Rich to see that I loved *him,* not his money. Which turned out to be dumb, because Rich didn't catch on to what I was trying to say."

I patted Tess' hand. "Anyway, after we split Rich kept up with the counseling and eventually he and Dina were able to make it up, and they got married again, which is great. And I found Joe, and I'm happy, too, so it all worked out."

It all worked out after a lot of heartburn, but I didn't go into that. I just pulled out my own phone and checked with my office, promising Aunt Nettie I'd get there sometime.

Tess sat quietly while I was on the phone, but as soon as I clicked off, she had another question.

"Lee, did you and Joe live together? Before you got married, I mean?"

Oh, ye gods! Was she going to ask me about the birds and the bees next?

"I never moved in with him," I said. "It just never was convenient. But we're normal people, Tess. We spent a lot of time together." I winked at her. "Planning our wedding."

She smiled. I looked across the room at Joe, and I noticed that he was holding his phone to his ear with his left hand, but he had covered his eyes with his right one. And he was shaking all over.

The rat! He was laughing at me.

I shook my finger at him. "And when Tess gets her gun back, I'm going to borrow it and shoot somebody. Right in the patootie."

Joe looked at me then, and we both began to laugh. Poor Tess was embarrassed. She excused herself and went to get some lunch. We were all tired of that hospital lunchroom, but she promised not to leave the building — even to go across the street for a hamburger.

As soon as we were alone, Joe came over, sat beside me, and gave me a real kiss. Then he spoke softly, right in my ear. "These kids just don't know anything about it, do they?"

"I guess they'll find out."

"At least you didn't tell her the first piece of furniture I ever bought was a king-size bed."

"I thought you needed that bed because you're tall."

"I had a tall girlfriend, too. With the old twin, I was always nervous about one of us landing on the floor at a crucial moment."

We stopped with the snuggling then, because after all we were in a public hospital waiting room, and we might be alone at the moment, but we could be interrupted anytime. And we were. Hogan came in.

He looked the area over. "Are any of these chairs comfortable?"

"The gray recliner's the best," Joe said. "Did you get anything out of the girl at Valk Souvenirs?"

"Nope. In fact, I didn't talk to her."

"Why not?"

"She's hightailed it. The place was deserted."

Chapter 19

After the big chase down Big Pine Road, naturally, Tess had made a statement, telling Hogan and the sheriff she had visited Valk Souvenirs before being chased by the SUV. The sheriff had obtained a search warrant and gone to the remote business. Hogan said he had gone along.

Now he looked rather discouraged. "Nothing there," he said. "No cars in the drive. No food in the kitchen. No clothes in the closet. A few boxes in the big barn, all empty."

Joe and I drooped at this report, and Tess was even droopier when she heard. We had all hoped that Hogan could give that dumb girl at Valk's a shot of truth serum — or something a little more practical and realistic — to get her to talk, and the whole mystery would be solved. We would know why Jeff had been attacked, why he had hidden in our attic, why Tess had been pursued, why the captain of *La Paloma* came to our house, who killed him, and why. We would learn the answers to all the little problems that had been pestering us.

No such luck. The suspects, such as the girl at Valk's, had flown the coop. The sheriff had checked on ownership of the site, but the landowners were being hard to find.

The four of us powwowed, but no ready solutions came to mind.

Jeff was sleeping, and Hogan still had an off-duty cop to keep him safe. I refrained from asking who was paying the fee for this. I knew the budget of the Warner Pier Police Department wouldn't cover it.

There was, of course, one more question for Tess — one that at Hogan's request, Joe and I had not asked. We were both longing to know the answer. Now Hogan did the honors.

"Young lady," he said, "last night when Captain Jacobs appeared at the door, Lee says he held out a package. Then he collapsed. Then the three of you — quite rightly — became more interested in his condition than in the package. But we need to know what happened to that package."

Tess sat very still. She didn't say anything.

Hogan's face was stern. "Apparently you took it. Where is it now?"

And Tess — sweet little Tess — balked. "I'm not saying anything," she said.

She sat back in her chair, set her jaw, and glared at Hogan as sternly as he was glaring at her.

The problem with this refusal to answer, of course, was that it was an answer. If Tess wasn't going to tell, there was some reason she wouldn't, and the reason was plain. She obviously had known all about the package.

Tess was such an innocent. It was impossible to get angry with her. The three of us stared at her. Her denial was a guilty plea.

Hogan began to laugh. Joe and I joined him.

"Don't laugh at me!" Tess sounded fierce. "I'm trying to help Jeff. I love him."

Hogan looked completely confused. Since he had missed the true-confessions session with Tess and Jeff pledging their undying love, I filled him in. I finished with a recap of the reasons Jeff had given, or partly given, for coming to Warner Pier.

"Jeff came up here looking for a replica of a falcon once owned by Mary Astor, or one that may have been — or maybe was not — used as a prop in the movie *The Maltese Falcon.*"

Tess looked as if she were going to cry. "He doesn't think it's a real falcon from the movie. He's not stupid!"

"We understand," Joe said. "It appears that Jeff is a good researcher, and he has been sensible about the whole thing. But the question now is, did Captain Jacobs have a package with him when he came to our house?"

Tess caved. "Well, yes," she said. "When you tried to give him CPR, and Lee ran for the telephone, you told me to stay in the house. But I saw the package lying there on the porch. I went out and asked if I could help. And, Joe, you said no. So I picked the package up and took it back in the house."

Hogan took over his own questioning. "Did you open it?"

"No."

I couldn't believe it. "Good night, Tess! How did you resist? I would have opened it in a New York minute!"

"I was afraid to! It might have been a bomb or something."

Hogan's voice was incredulous. "So you kept it in your room overnight and took it to the hospital first thing in the morning? That makes a huge amount of sense."

"I wanted to ask Jeff what to do with it."

Hogan raised his eyebrows. "Then you and Jeff opened it."

"Well. Yes, we did."

"What was in it?"

"I'd rather Jeff told you. But it wasn't anything important! He just laughed when he saw it. Then he told me to put it in a safe place."

"After someone had been killed?"

"Well . . ." Tess tried the eyelash flickering again. "I didn't tell him about that."

"So, where did you put it?" Hogan asked.

Tess' lips became a thin line. She sat back in her chair, crossed her arms, and didn't say a word.

We all gave her the glare treatment, but she didn't say anything. And she didn't cry. In a way, I was proud of her for holding her ground, but I sure did want to know what was in that package. Besides, withholding that information was dangerous.

"In the book and the movie," I said, "Sam Spade puts the bird in a locker at a bus station and mails himself the key."

That didn't tempt Tess into saying anything either.

We all stared for a minute longer. Then I turned to Hogan. "Are you going to arrest her?" I asked.

"Not yet. I'll let her examine her conscience a little longer. But I sure have grounds. Obstruction of justice, for one thing."

I turned to Joe. "Can you take me home? If I'm not doing any good here, I'd better go to the office."

Joe nodded and stood up. We walked toward the elevator, leaving Hogan to deal with Tess. He had the authority to do something about her lack of cooperation, and we didn't. Her car was being examined by the forensics folks, so Hogan would have to be responsible for getting her back to our house. We stopped for a quick hamburger and hit the road for home.

Only one strange thing happened. As we got out of the elevator on the ground floor of the hospital, I saw someone. It wasn't anyone I knew. In fact, I wasn't sure I saw the guy at all; he popped up and then disappeared like a Texas prairie dog jumping into his hole.

But I stopped in my tracks. Joe walked on. I whispered his name, but he didn't hear me.

So I went into a rapid trot until I could catch up with him. "Joe, did you see that guy in the hat?"

He stopped and turned toward me. "Hat? What kind of hat?"

"It looked like a fedora, only made of straw, with a wide band."

"Some out-of-towner here for your festival?"

"I don't know." I looked back the way I had come, but there were about a dozen people standing around the elevator, and the man I'd seen wasn't one of them.

"He was a scrawny kind of guy," I said. "Thin. Colorless."

"Why did you notice him?"

"I feel as if I've seen him before. But I don't know where."

Joe scanned the crowd. "Do you see him now?"

I shook my head.

"There were a lot of fedoras at the yacht club party. Could he have been there, or at the tour of the yacht?"

"Maybe. But most of those hats were felt."

"We'd better head home, Lee."

I mulled it over on the way home. As we turned off the interstate I finally spoke. "Joe, this whole situation is stupid! It seems as if it's an elaborate scheme to fool Jeff into buying some fake falcon. But Jeff's too knowledgeable for that."

"But the crooks — if they are crooks — may not know that Jeff hasn't been fooled. They apparently think he could still be enticed into buying the falcon, believing it would win Grossman's prize."

"Which still wouldn't explain why someone's chasing all over the country after Jeff, and after the package Captain Jacobs had."

Joe shrugged. "They must believe that whatever is in the package is really valuable."

"Huh! Nothing in this whole deal is as valuable as Jeff."

I'd blurted the words out, but as I heard myself say them, I saw that they were true. Talk about your lightbulb moments.

Joe spoke, but I didn't even hear him. He had to tap me on the arm before I took in what he had said.

"What do you mean, Lee?"

"Two people have told us that a Maltese Falcon prop sold for more than four million dollars. But, Joe, do you know how much Jeff is worth to his dad?"

I leaned toward Joe and spoke as distinctly as I could. "Much more than four million."

Joe flipped his head toward me, and the truck swerved. "Four million? Are you saying that Rich is worth four million dollars?"

"Heck, Joe! He's worth a lot more than that. Twenty million? More? I don't know. Rich would never tell me anything about his finances. But I can read a tax return when you leave one out on the coffee table, and I know that Rich Godfrey Enterprises owns — well, a lot. And that Rich himself has a sensible attitude about debt. He's not highly leveraged. The technical term for Rich's net worth is 'rolling in it.' "

"And you walked out on him and refused a financial settlement? If I had been your lawyer, I would never have let you do that! You had rights, Lee."

"I didn't want them. And my lawyer tried. He did make Rich pay all the costs of the divorce. And he paid for six months of counseling sessions for me." I paused. "The best thing I can say about Rich is that he's a self-made man. Or nearly. He did start with an inheritance, but he's made it grow twenty times."

"Sometimes I'm amazed by your attitude. I mean, I never before ran into an efficient and effective businesswoman — with a degree in accounting, no less — who doesn't seem to know the value of money."

"Oh, I know the value! If Rich taught me anything, it was that if you think everything, including love, can be measured in dollars and cents, any money you have is more of a nightmare than a benefit. I found it frightening. I told you, I used to worry all the time when I had to ferry Jeff around Dallas. Especially if he'd wander off in a mall or someplace. Neither Jeff nor Rich had any conception that he might be a target for kidnappers."

"Maybe there wasn't anything to worry about."

"I thought there was! If a strange man had stopped Jeff on the street and said, 'Young man, help me look for my dog,' Jeff would have climbed right into his car. And his dad was very offhand about dangers, too. When I tried to talk to Rich about it, he just shrugged. He'd say, 'There are lots of guys in Dallas richer than I am. My protection is that we don't throw our money around. Money is to make more money.' He actually thought that!"

"He wanted to reinvest, not live lavishly."

"Yes. He called that living on an inconspicuous scale. Of course, then he'd get in his Lamborghini and drive off. Like no one would notice his twenty-thousand-dollar watch."

Joe sat silently for about a mile, then spoke. "I guess I never realized what you gave up for me."

"Don't let it go to your head. I didn't give it up for you! I gave it up for me! But why would you be impressed? You were married to one of the most famous women in the country."

"Yeah, but she didn't have that kind of

money. And the life we lived got to be miserable."

"The life I lived with Rich wasn't any fun either."

Joe didn't say anything else. He just reached across the seat and took my hand. "I'm a lucky guy," he said.

"We're both lucky," I said. "If only because we don't have to worry about either of us getting kidnapped. But, Joe, if I were going to try to get money out of Jeff Godfrey, I wouldn't mess around with falcons. I'd hold him for ransom."

I was becoming furious with the people who were doing threatening things to us, who had apparently attacked Jeff and had killed Captain Jacobs. These unknown bad guys had turned our lives upside down. Joe and I were both running around, looking out for Jeff, looking out for Tess, dealing with corpses on our front porch, calling Alicia, snatching meals in fast-food restaurants, and generally not getting our own lives taken care of.

I was sick and tired of the whole thing.

Well, I wasn't going to let them — whoever "them" was — run my life any longer. I vowed that when I finally got to the office, I was going to do something I wanted to do, or at least something I needed to do.

So when we got to the house, I changed clothes and slapped on some makeup. In ten minutes, I had pulled my hair into a George Washington queue and had limped back out the door, headed for the office.

I yelled good-bye to Joe. "I'll see you sometime!"

It was quite a letdown when I got to TenHuis Chocolade and nobody seemed to need me.

I went to my office, propped my crutch behind the desk, and looked things over. It was after four o'clock. The tourists were buying truffles and bonbons, and the counter girls were selling them. The workroom seemed to be moving efficiently. Aunt Nettie was showing the newest employee how to "spout," which is chocolatier talk for using a funnel to fill bonbon shells. Dolly was rolling ganache into centers for truffles.

I took time to nibble a key lime truffle ("white chocolate filling flavored with key lime, enrobed with dark chocolate, and embellished with a green dot"). I felt unneeded.

I turned to the mail. Even that looked routine. I sorted the orders into one pile and the bills into another. Then I looked over the orders that had come in by computer, but going through those didn't seem appealing.

All this made me really feel let down. I had to face facts. Despite my moment of truth on the way back from Holland, I didn't *want* to do my regular work and live my regular life. I wanted to know what was going on, why all these crazy things had happened to me and Joe, to Jeff, and to Tess. I was ashamed of myself, but there it was. I wanted to find the villains, to solve the crimes.

When I looked up, I saw that Aunt Nettie had finished her spouting demonstration and was coming toward my office. I knew she'd want a full report on our adventure with Tess. And I didn't want to talk about that. I wanted to do something about it.

So when Aunt Nettie walked into my office, I spoke before she could. "Let's go deliver chocolates," I said.

"Where do we need to deliver them?"

"To *La Paloma.* I promised to take Mr. Grossman a box of the chocolate falcons, and I haven't done it."

Chapter 20

It was, or so Aunt Nettie and I were told later, a stupid thing to do. But we weren't completely dumb about it.

First, Aunt Nettie was as eager to go as I was. She and I might not be blood relatives, but we somehow had identical curiosity genes. So we were sticking together.

Second, we called Hogan and left a message on his cell phone, telling him what we were doing. We also told Dolly Jolly — and Dolly could get results.

We drove to the yacht club, gambling that we'd find a parking space. Some of the handicapped slots there were usually open, at least when there wasn't a big party going on, and I had a handicapped permit. Besides, we probably wouldn't be going onto the yacht. We'd just send our chocolates over by rowboat.

The parking worked out as planned. And, unexpectedly, there was no need for a rowboat to get aboard *La Paloma.* She had been moved.

The yacht club marina had found a dockside berth for her. No longer did we have to climb down a ladder, climb into a rowboat, be rowed out into the river, and then climb onto the swim platform to get onto the yacht. Now we merely crossed to the main deck by the gangway.

Everything was simple as pie, except one thing. I didn't have any idea why we had come, and Aunt Nettie was only there because I'd asked her to come with me. Why did I want to pay a call on the Grossman yacht? What did I think I might learn there? Would I hand over the chocolate falcons and leave?

Noel Kayro greeted us. He was wearing his 1930s outfit, a dark suit complete with vest, plus spats. He waved us onto the yacht.

"How is Jeff?" he asked.

"He's improving," I said. "I'll tell him you're in the area as soon as the doctors okay it. But look at you! You're all dressed for the big event this evening." The showing of *The Maltese Falcon* was scheduled for eight o'clock.

"Yes. Ready for business," Kayro said. "The business of my hobby."

A big bass voice boomed behind us. "Ah,

Mrs. Woodyard."

I turned and greeted Grossman. He was also wearing his role-playing outfit, the 1930s yachting togs.

"And this is my aunt," I said, "Nettie TenHuis Jones. She is the chocolatier deluxe for TenHuis Chocolade." I held out the box of chocolate falcons I had brought along. "And here are the falcons I promised you."

Grossman's face lit up. He eagerly took the box of chocolates, slipped off the blue ribbon, and opened it. I had the feeling he was going to devour the whole box without even offering it around. That action would have been strictly out of character for Kasper Gutman, the character he was portraying. Gutman was always suave and polite, even when he was ordering a murder.

Grossman restrained himself, however, and politely offered falcons to the rest of us. Aunt Nettie and I declined, but Kayro took one. Then Grossman helped himself. His "Delicious!" was extremely enthusiastic. The falcons, of course, were solid chocolate, not filled with exotically flavored ganache. But their smooth creaminess was worth a few slobbers.

I did come up with at least one question. "I had another motive for coming," I said. "Naturally I'm shocked by the death of

Captain Jacobs. And I'm sure the police have questioned everybody on *La Paloma.* I wondered if you had been told anything about the crime."

"No, we've been given no news," Grossman said. "Except that he died on your veranda. I deeply regret that you had such a horrifying experience."

"I had not had the pleasure of meeting the captain, unfortunately." I was beginning to talk like Grossman myself. "Joe, my husband, was horrified; he had had a chance to become slightly acquainted with Captain Jacobs. And for those of you who knew him well, the blow must have been much worse."

Grossman frowned. "I have to admit that I barely knew Jacobs myself." He stopped talking and glanced at Kayro.

There was a brief silence. Then Kayro spoke. "The captain was employed through an agency. He had just joined the crew on this trip."

"Oh! So he wasn't a close associate," I said.

"Not an associate at all," Grossman said. He puffed himself up slightly, seeming to regain confidence. "I flew out to meet *La Paloma* here in Warner Pier. The captain and I met for the first time then. We had barely spoken before that."

"If Captain Jacobs didn't know anyone in the Warner Pier area, or even on *La Paloma,* it seems really strange that anyone would harm him here."

"Like you, I fail to understand how this could happen," Grossman said.

Aunt Nettie gave her face a sweet-little-old-lady expression. "So the police have no idea who might have killed him?" She made it a question.

"They have not shared any information with us," Grossman said.

"I haven't been able to get a word out of Hogan either," Aunt Nettie said.

Grossman and Kayro both looked mystified, so I explained, "My aunt is married to our chief of police, Hogan Jones."

Grossman's eyes widened, making him look almost frightened, and Kayro chuckled nervously. "I hope you haven't come as your husband's emissary," he said.

"Oh no. I'm just a regular Warner Pier person," Aunt Nettie said. "Everyone here is crazy about boats."

After that strong hint, of course we got a tour. This time, despite my crutch, I climbed all over the yacht. I saw the master stateroom and the three guest staterooms, the crew quarters, the bridge, the exercise room, the upper and lower decks, and the kitchen.

The kitchen was occupied by the only crew member we saw. This was a plain young woman wearing a large white jacket and with a large white cap covering her hair. She was chopping onions, and all we could see of her was red eyes and a runny nose. She glared as we came in, and answered Aunt Nettie's questions about cooking on a boat gruffly. Apparently she found it annoying to stop and be pleasant to visitors while doing a chore that made her feel unattractive. Or maybe she was unpleasant all the time.

Grossman introduced her as Rae, the cook.

I smiled. "But, Mr. Grossman, Rae should be your daughter."

"My daughter? I'm afraid I am childless, Mrs. Woodyard."

"Ah, but in *The Maltese Falcon* novel, Gutman's daughter, Rhea, entices Sam Spade away from the main scene of the action at the crucial time. But perhaps her name is pronounced Ree-ah, rather than Ray-ah."

Grossman smiled. "We're not complete purists," he said.

This evidence of the existence of crew members made me turn to Grossman. "Will you sail the yacht back to Buffalo yourself?"

He gave me that wide-eyed, almost frightened look again. "Oh no! We have contacted the agency asking for a temporary captain. The crew will take the boat back. I must return more rapidly. By air. Though I knew Captain Jacobs only slightly, I feel that I must speak with his family. In fact, I'm leaving early tomorrow."

I resisted making a comment, but I did wonder why he owned a multimillion-dollar yacht when he apparently never sailed in it.

We left the yacht then, with Aunt Nettie effusively thanking Grossman for the tour, and Grossman effusively thanking her for the truffles. I hope I was polite, but I mainly concentrated on limping back across the gangway.

I was getting tired, and I still had to cross the park. But I made it to the van and climbed behind the steering wheel.

Once we were settled, I turned to Aunt Nettie. "Well, that little tour provided quite a bit of fodder for questions."

"It certainly did," she said. "Especially the cook."

"Why her in particular?"

"Lee! Didn't you recognize her?"

"I guess not. Who was she?"

"She was the same girl we talked to out at Valk's!"

"Oh no!" I stared at Aunt Nettie, completely stunned. "That can't be!"

"Oh yes," she said. "I'm sure she was the same girl."

"Oshawna Bridges? Are you sure?"

"Well, I was when we were on board," Aunt Nettie said. "The onions were a nice touch. There's nothing like crying to make you look different. It changes the expression."

"Yes, and the cap helped, now that I think about it. Her black ringlets were the most distinctive thing about her out at Valk's. I was mesmerized by them. But that cap she's wearing now covers every curl. And it's quicker than a dye job. Or the ringlets could have been a wig in the first place."

I pictured the cook again, then thought about the Valk girl. "Aunt Nettie, I think you're right. It *was* her."

"We must tell Hogan. She may be in danger."

"Oh. Then you think she's being held on the yacht against her will."

"It seems like a strong possibility to me, Lee. Remember how cowed she seemed when we met her out at Valk's?"

"I guess that's possible. At any rate, we

also need to watch the yacht. If Grossman or Kayro realized or if she realized herself that we've figured out who she is . . . well, she could really be in danger. Or she could take off. Neither situation is good."

"Do you have your cell phone? Do you want to call Hogan? Or shall I?"

"We shouldn't be too obvious. They may be watching us. So? How about a drink?"

"A drink?"

"The main film festival action tonight is over at the theater. So Kayro and Grossman, and maybe Oshawna Bridges as well, should be hanging around the yacht, getting ready to go to the movies. The yacht club bar shouldn't be crowded, and we can still see the yacht from the window. We could make a phone call from there. If one of them leaves, we should see them."

"I think that's a good plan, Lee."

So we got back out of the van and walked — I hobbled — across the park to the yacht club. We went in, sat down in a corner, and ordered coffee. I called Hogan. It took three full minutes and a lot of dramatic whispering using words like "vital" and "he must know" and "imperative that we reach him" before his assistant agreed to find him for us. We were still drinking our coffee when Hogan called us back.

Then, of course, he wasn't sure he should believe us. I handed the phone to Aunt Nettie, and she was able to convince him.

She punched the OFF button. "He told me we should leave here and go back to the shop," she said.

I nodded, climbed aboard my crutch, and limped back to the van. As in most vans, in mine the front row of seating had two separate seats with a console between them. I got into the driver's seat, keeping my mouth shut as Aunt Nettie climbed into the passenger's seat. But as soon as the doors were closed and my seat belt was fastened, I spoke.

"I hope Hogan gets Miss Bridges settled quickly, because I want to talk to him about the whole atmosphere out there."

Aunt Nettie clicked her seat belt. "You mentioned that earlier," she said. "I wasn't sure what you meant."

I inserted the key in the ignition and went on talking. "It's just an odd situation. That's supposed to be Grossman's yacht, but Kayro almost seems to be in charge."

"Oh!" Aunt Nettie yelped loudly, and I whirled to look at her. "What's wrong?" Then I gave a loud "Oh!" of my own.

A huge automatic pistol had materialized between us.

And now a head appeared. A head wearing a straw fedora.

I wanted to laugh. The whole thing seemed to be a joke, some sort of prank dealing with *The Maltese Falcon.*

"What's going on?" I asked.

"Just start the van and back out." The command came in a tinny little voice.

"Who are you?" I asked. "And what do you want?"

"Forget the questions. Just back out and drive where I tell you. Or your aunt gets it!"

I stared at the person between us, but all I could see was the top and brim of a fedora. I kept trying to take in the situation. I couldn't.

Aunt Nettie spoke. "Young man, I suggest you get out of the van and go your way," she said. "I cannot believe you would actually fire a pistol here, on the busiest street in a busy resort, thronged with people. That would be silly."

"Try me!" The man's voice sounded desperate.

Aunt Nettie gave a deep sigh and unhooked her seat belt. "I refuse to cooperate with such a foolish business," she said.

"Really, Aunt Nettie," I said. "We got so worried about Gutman, Cairo, and Bridget that we forgot about Wilmer."

Then I pulled the keys out of the ignition and hit the alarm attached to my key chain.

All hell broke loose.

CHAPTER 21

When I pushed the alarm button, and all kinds of noise exploded, our intruder threw the door open. The van's parking place, of course, was wide because it was a handicapped slot. The man dressed as the character "Wilmer" left the door gaping open and walked rapidly away, headed into the crowded park.

I opened my door and stood up in it, waving my arms wildly and pointing at the guy in the fedora. He had the sense to look at me as if I were a lunatic and to keep walking. Naturally everybody in the area thought Aunt Nettie or I had hit an alarm accidentally. They stood around staring at us, but nobody *did* anything.

I suppose that — if I'd been thinking quickly — I would have turned off the alarm, screamed like mad, and followed Mr. Fedora down the street. Later Hogan said it was a good thing I didn't do that.

"An action that threatening might have forced him to use the gun," he said. "The idea is to keep yourself out of danger."

So Aunt Nettie and I were not hurt or kidnapped. And we thanked our lucky stars for that.

The worst part of the whole adventure was that during the excitement, the cook, whoever she was, disappeared from the yacht. I was so proud of Aunt Nettie for spotting her, and then the girl zapped herself into the ether.

After Hogan had checked on the crazy ladies in the van with the alarm blaring, she was gone, and of course, neither Noel Kayro nor Grossman admitted to seeing her go. They claimed to have no idea what had happened to her.

Bah! I would have been happy to shove them both overboard. Right off the luxury yacht and into the Warner River. At its deepest, muddiest point.

But they claimed they had run to the rail when they heard our alarm go off. And after that, Rae the cook was gone. Maybe she went overboard.

Aunt Nettie still feared the girl was being kept prisoner in the bilges, if yachts have bilges, but Hogan said Grossman let him look everywhere on the boat, and there was no sign of her.

Hogan had given Aunt Nettie and me his obligatory lectures on taking risks — "Yes, dear." "I understand, Hogan." — when we finally realized there were two passengers in Hogan's official car.

He had brought Tess back to Warner Pier, along with — ta-da! — Jeff.

Joe had arrived by then, and he and I greeted Jeff effusively, but I'm afraid my first thought on seeing him had actually been less welcoming.

I said it out loud as soon as I had Joe alone. "Oh, Joe! How are we going to keep that kid safe?"

"I already asked Hogan. He's going to have a guard on duty at our house. I talked to him and explained your theory of Jeff being the possible target of kidnappers."

"I suppose he had already figured it out."

"I think learning that Jeff's dad is actually an extremely wealthy man reinforced some ideas he already had. Maybe. Anyway, from now on Jeff's to have bodyguards."

"I guess he'll have to. But that'll mean having three houseguests and only two guest rooms."

"The bodyguards will not require a bedroom, Lee. Or even meals, if you don't want to provide them."

"Don't be silly! I'm the granddaughter of Susanna McKinney and the niece by marriage of Nettie TenHuis Jones. I can't have people in the house and not *feed* them."

Joe laughed. "I'll order pizza tonight." Then he spoke in my ear. "And what makes you think Tess and Jeff will need two guest rooms?"

"I guess upstairs will be off-limits for you and me the next few days," I said. "I don't want to know anything at all about what's going on up there. I still think of Jeff as about fourteen years old and Tess as twelve!"

I phoned Alicia Richardson with the joyful news that Jeff was out of the hospital. She still hadn't reached Jeff's parents, but she seemed to be calmed by speaking to him in person. At least she had quit threatening to get on a plane and fly up to take command.

So the whole crew was at our house for dinner. Aunt Nettie brought ice cream and chocolates, and Tess insisted on providing bags of salad. Joe picked up the pizza. All I had to do was set the table and remember where I'd stored the great big paper napkins.

We had a festive meal, though we had to keep reminding one another that Jeff was supposed to stay quiet. He said he felt fine, but he still didn't remember how he had gotten into our attic.

The bodyguard was the one I'd played gin with in the hospital waiting room. I finally thought to ask his name, and it was Duane. And his last name was McKinney! We called each other cousin from then on, though he admitted he had no relatives who lived outside Michigan, and all my McKinney kinfolks had moved to Texas from Kentucky before the Civil War.

"I'm sure we're shirttail relatives," I said.

"Maybe so, though my dad always said all his relatives were hanged."

"Definitely the same family," Joe said. "Have another piece of pizza, Duane."

Hogan provided one more surprise: Tess' car. The crime lab was through with it, and he had one of the patrolmen bring it out. He also quietly slipped her pistol to her. This time it was in a lockbox.

After dinner Hogan and Aunt Nettie went home. Duane and Joe walked around outside, making sure Duane had a clear idea of where vehicles, yard lights, and other paraphernalia were. Joe also made sure Duane had keys to the outside doors. Duane assured us he would sit up in the living room all night. And, yes, he was accustomed to sitting in the quiet. He'd be fine, he said.

Then we went to bed. Jeff and Tess upstairs — and I was still vowing to stay away from up there — and Joe and me downstairs. Thank goodness we'd added an upstairs bathroom.

As he went up, Jeff said he felt "a little shaky," but he kissed me on the cheek and thanked us.

"Just think," he said. "One of the main things I wanted to do on this trip was take you all to dinner to show you how much I appreciated your help four years ago. And here you are, taking care of me again."

"No problem!"

"I know I've been a pain in the neck. I hope things are looking up. I'll have to see about my car tomorrow. I don't even know where it is."

"No hurry," I said. "The car is safe. Sleep late and take it easy."

Then I got into my own bed and tried to figure what the heck was going on. Because something was, and it wasn't just a case of a misplaced statue.

I had brought my laptop with me, and by the time Joe got into his pajamas I was deep in a spreadsheet.

Joe looked over my shoulder, then lay down, stared at the ceiling, and spoke. "Okay. I assume you're not working on next year's budget for TenHuis Chocolade."

"Nope. I'm figuring out how much money these crooks have spent handing out trouble over the past week."

"It's more than a week. The Valk Web site began to work on Jeff a couple of months ago."

"True." I flopped onto my stomach and looked into Joe's ear. "So. You agree this was a kidnapping scheme?"

"Very possibly."

"I think the scam over the supposedly valuable falcon statue was definitely a blind. Jeff tumbled on that right away."

"What does your spreadsheet indicate as the bad guys' investment so far?"

"Motel rooms, gasoline, meals, possibly airline tickets. Plus the biggest potential item: rental of the yacht, though Grossman may actually own the yacht. And staff. They've had to pay out a major sum on this scheme. Even if the con job over the fake falcon were to work, I don't see how they could make much money. But the real mystery is Captain Jacobs. He's really dead, Joe. Why did they have to kill him?"

"We'll never know until one of them tells us." Joe sighed.

"I don't think he was part of it. I think

they hired him from an agency, just like they said."

"Yes, he must not have been one of the baddies. He probably figured out that something was wrong. Then he had to pay."

I took Joe's hand. I knew how bad he felt about Jacobs' death. "And he must have wanted to tell you."

"Maybe. At least, I don't see any other reason for his showing up on our front porch. But why me? We had barely met. Why not go to the police?"

"I don't know." I squeezed Joe's hand, then leaned against the headboard and propped my boot up on a couple of pillows.

"So, I'll try to recap." I cleared my throat importantly. "Several weeks ago someone who either knows Jeff or knows a lot about Jeff uses the Falcone Web site to introduce Jeff to the idea that he could make a lot of money by finding this unknown falcon."

"Maybe Jeff had already talked about going to the Warner Pier Film Festival."

"That might be it. Because Jeff may be inexperienced, but he's not an idiot, and he wouldn't have been chatting about his romantic problems with a stranger. And his love life is key to why he wanted money."

"Agreed."

"Anyway, the crooks — and I'm not sure

who's a crook and who isn't, but I suspect Kayro — come to our area and find a remote property to rent. They also rent or borrow the yacht and have it sailed around from Buffalo."

"Of course, they may not have planned to pay more than the deposit on yacht rental."

"Oh, wow! I hadn't thought of that. Stiffing the yacht owner would save a lot of money. Anyway, they hire the yacht and a crew to bring it over here. But Jeff accidentally fools the crooks. He comes to Warner Pier on his own, without confiding in Kayro, and meets up with me."

Joe turned over to face me, and we both nodded. "I feel certain Kayro had no idea Jeff had relatives in this area," I said. "I'm guessing that from his surprise when I mentioned Jeff's name at the motel."

"I think you're right."

"To make things worse, Jeff finds the so-called Valk property on his own. And that could nearly have demolished the plan. They were probably preparing to spring the trap a day or so later and wham! Jeff shows up — I suspect — before they're ready for him."

"And he must have shown up at a time when there was nobody there but that girl."

"Right. Miss Oshawna Bridges, originally

Miss Bridget O'Shaughnessy, as created by Dashiell Hammett. The plot required that Jeff be lured out there, and that they imprison him in that cabin."

"An ideal location for holding a kidnapping victim."

"But Oshawna can't overpower Jeff on her own, so they have to improvise. Oshawna gets hold of Wilmer or Kayro — I can't see Grossman in this role — and they start looking for Jeff. They force Jeff's car off the road, and he receives a head injury."

"But Jeff once again gets away," Joe said. "He's able to get to our house. He remembers where the key was hidden and gets inside."

"That explains why he hid in the attic!" I said. "He wasn't thinking straight because of the concussion, but he knew someone was after him, so he hid in the attic. Ye gods! The kid has an amazing instinct for self-preservation! And thanks to Tess' plot to bug his car, and to his cell phone, we were able to find him before he dried up into a mummy. Then Hogan had the smarts to put him in the hospital under an alias. So the gang hasn't been able to get close to him since."

I tapped Joe on the shoulder. "And that has foiled their kidnapping plan."

"I don't see what else it could be. Since you finally mentioned that Jeff's dad is much wealthier than I had visualized."

We both mulled that over for at least a full minute. Then I spoke again. "I feel as if I should take a quilt upstairs and sleep in front of Jeff's door."

"Not a good idea, Lee! Two young adults who are in love and in adjoining bedrooms? Damn tactless, these stepmothers."

"Damn worried! And in adjoining bedrooms, my foot!"

We were both quiet for another minute. "Sorry," I said, "but I don't like having Jeff loose up here in Michigan. The bad guys could still be after him."

"That's why Duane is sitting in the living room. And as soon as the doctors approve, Jeff and Tess are both on a plane for Dallas, okay?"

"Okay." I sighed deeply and began to close out the laptop. "I know this is all just speculation. The real explanation may be entirely different."

"Right," Joe said. "The real question is, how is Hogan going to prove anything?"

We turned out the light.

If my life were a suspense novel — which it sometimes resembles — we would have awakened the next morning to find Jeff and

Tess had both disappeared. But no, both were there and ready for bacon and eggs. Duane was fine, too. He was relieved by a fellow named Bob at eight a.m. Bob had already eaten, but accepted coffee.

The day seemed to be starting well. I breathed a sigh of relief.

I breathed that sigh too early, of course. It wasn't until two that afternoon that anyone was kidnapped.

CHOCOLATE CHAT

This recipe defines what fudge is for my family. I'm sure my grandmother did not originate the recipe, but it makes wonderful, smooth fudge without a whole lot of beating.

Some people like a crumblier fudge. They may prefer the Hershey's version earlier in the book.

GRAN'S FUDGE

4 1/2 cups sugar
1 large can evaporated milk
18 ounces chocolate chips
1 pint jar marshmallow cream
2 tablespoons butter or margarine
1 teaspoon vanilla extract
dash salt
2 cups pecans

Cook sugar and evaporated milk to soft ball stage. (Boil at least ten minutes, then drop a bit into cold water. When it's ready, the drop will form a soft ball when rolled between fingertips.) Add chocolate chips, marshmallow cream, butter, vanilla, salt, and pecans. Mix well. Pour into buttered dish. Let set for 24 hours before cutting.

Chapter 22

Of course, as we ate breakfast we didn't know the day was going to be as full of threats and thrills as any noir movie. No, we talked about mundane things.

Tess was delighted to have her car back, and Jeff was eager to get a look at his. Joe, who was the only one of us who had seen the car, warned him that the damage was extensive.

"It may be totaled," he said. "Whoever wrecked it ran it right off into the woods and into a ravine. Who carries your insurance?"

Jeff found his insurance cards, and they called the Dallas insurance agent to tell him what had happened. Joe promised me he'd help Jeff get action under way and would not let him become too exhausted by the process.

As we finished eating, Hogan showed up. He accepted a cup of coffee, and the six of us sat around the breakfast table while he gave us instructions. That was when Jeff and Tess first heard about the possibility of a kidnapping plot.

Tears welled up in Tess' eyes, but she didn't say anything.

Jeff blustered, "That's stupid! My dad wouldn't give a nickel for ransom. Not for me. It can't be true!"

We all ignored that remark. Obviously Rich would give every cent he had in the world if Jeff were in danger. And in his heart, Jeff knew that.

Hogan kept talking. "A kidnapping plot makes more sense than thinking someone simply tried to kill you, Jeff. Unless you're involved with some activity that would tempt someone to blow you away?"

Jeff looked mystified. "What do you mean?"

"Have you been selling drugs?" Hogan asked. "Robbing banks? Drugging women at parties?"

"No! I wouldn't do anything like that. I lead a dull life. I volunteer at the museum. I swim a couple of times a week. I work in an antiques shop, for God's sake! And I sell movie memorabilia. Tess is the only thing interesting in my life. There's no reason for anybody to kill me."

"But those things happened. If nobody wants to kill you, it could be they wanted to kidnap you."

Jeff frowned, but he didn't say anything more.

Hogan spoke firmly. "Kidnapping makes more sense than anything else, Jeff. I want all of us to act as if it's true. Now, this doesn't mean you have to sit in your room surrounded by armed guards. No, we want to fool these guys, make them think none of us suspects anything. If they come up and speak to you, try to act normal. For example, this Noel Kayro claims to be a friend of yours."

"There was a volunteer at the museum, Hal, who did a Joel Cairo impersonation," Jeff said. "I wouldn't say we were close friends, but I worked with him. Sometimes we had coffee or something."

"I think that's the guy who's here for the festival. He may be on the up-and-up, but he could be in with the bad guys. Now, I assume you'd like to go to the film festival. If Kayro wants to talk to you there, can you respond the way you would normally?"

"I can try."

"Good! If you have trouble, tell him all about your concussion. Blame that. In fact, it would be good to tell him you've lost your memory."

"Which I have. Pieces of it."

"I know. But play it up big. And treat the rest of the group the same way. Grossman and the girl, whatever name she's using today. Act as if you don't suspect anything.

"And, Tess?" Hogan shifted his attention. "Can you act normally?"

"I can try," she said. "If it will help catch them."

"Good girl! But if Kayro or anybody else wants you to wander off with them, don't go!"

We all laughed at the thought of wandering off with a potential kidnapper.

"Don't laugh!" Hogan's voice was firm. "Be cautious. It's like telling children not to get into cars with strangers. If someone comes up to a child and says, 'Your mother sent me. I'm supposed to bring you home,' children don't see the guy as a stranger. Experiments have shown that most kids will get right in the guy's car. Jeff, you're not dumb, but if they try to entice you away, they'll have a plausible story. Maybe 'Tess needs to talk to you' or 'You've got a phone call from your mom.' Savvy?"

We all nodded solemnly, and Hogan went on. "Don't even walk across the room to buy a Coke with one of these guys. And don't drink a Coke, or even a glass of water, one of them brings you. Don't fall for it."

I think he put a scare into all of us. Anyway, he made me think.

As soon as Hogan left, Joe and Jeff took off to see about the car. Bodyguard Bob went along.

Tess was fretting to go, too, but settled for doing a little laundry and pacing the floor. However, Jeff and Joe and Bob were back by noon. Jeff shook his head at the state of his Lexus, but the adjuster was to take a look at it that afternoon, and Jeff had been able to get some of his belongings out of the trunk.

"Hey, Tess!" he said. "My merchandise is okay. Maybe I can open up a booth at the film festival."

"Great! But I don't want you to work too hard."

"I may not be able to afford to deal," Jeff said. "If the booths are expensive . . . well, there's no point in losing money. I didn't bring very much stock."

I called to check on the price of a small booth, and Jeff decided it wasn't too high. The dealers' room was to open at one o'clock, and Mary Kay McCurley said she'd put Jeff's name on a table.

So Jeff, impatiently claiming he wasn't

tired, left for the film festival, this time accompanied by Tess and Bodyguard Bob.

Tess and Jeff seemed to be content, but I wasn't. I wanted to know what Hogan was doing about arresting this bunch of con men and crooks who, we believed, had come to Warner Pier with a complicated plan. First, they were trying to make money by fooling a young collector and dealer. Next, they were trying to make a lot more money by kidnapping him.

Naturally I tried asking Joe if he knew what was going on. He merely pleaded innocent.

"Lee, I feel sure something is going on. If Hogan sees danger to Jeff, he's not going to stand by and let it happen. But he hasn't confided in me."

With everybody else gone, I decided to go to the office. Which was useless, as it turned out. I was so keyed up about what was going on elsewhere that I got no work done. I just ate a chocolate malt truffle ("milk chocolate filling rolled in a milk chocolate shell and decorated with a dusting of malt cocoa"). Then I sulked and felt sorry for myself.

Finally, about three o'clock, I gave up and told Aunt Nettie and Dolly Jolly I was going to check in on the film festival. I made up a box of four truffles for Mary Kay. She'd mentioned she was partial to the combination of chocolate and ginger, so I picked two Asian Spice ("milk chocolate inside and out, with a dusting of ground ginger") and two Ginger Wasabi ("dark chocolate filling enrobed with more dark chocolate and embellished with crystallized ginger").

The film festival was being held at the Warner Point Convention Center. This center had originated as a house built by Joe's first wife, Clementine Ripley, a nationally known defense attorney. When she died without signing a new will, her entire estate went to Joe, who was also named executor.

Joe did not receive the property joyfully. In fact, he was mad as hops and considered the inheritance a pain in the — well, in the patootie.

At the time Clementine Ripley died, she and Joe had been divorced for two years, but some of their property issues had not been settled. Joe had been trying to break any final ties with her. He and I had just met, and he told me at the time that having her very complicated estate dropped into his lap was a nightmare. Simply refusing to accept the property wasn't legally practical, so he had to step in and settle things, but he resented it.

Among her holdings was the Warner Point property, located on a peninsula extending out into Lake Michigan. This included acres of valuable lakefront land, a large house, and several smaller buildings. It was worth millions, but it was also heavily mortgaged. It took another two years for Joe to get the property free and clear. He then presented it to the City of Warner Pier on the condition that his name never be publicly disclosed as the donor. He said he just didn't want to think about it ever again.

Lots of people knew the story, naturally, since there are no secrets in a town the size of Warner Pier. But most folks were polite enough not to mention the situation to either of us.

The city made the property into a convention and workshop center. A small auditorium was added to make it useful for meetings, and it now attracted many small conferences each year.

It had a good restaurant as well, but Joe didn't like to eat there. The property was an unhappy memory to him.

But that afternoon Warner Point had a festive air, although its main decorations were black-and-white posters of movie stars of the thirties and forties garbed as private eyes and gangsters.

The memorabilia dealers were set up in a room off the lobby of the theater. The films, of course, were being shown in the theater itself.

As I limped across the parking lot, someone called out, "Lee! Mrs. Woodyard!"

Looking around, I saw Noel Kayro falling in beside me. I gulped. I was facing one of the suspected bad guys. Could I do as Hogan had instructed us? Could I act as if I didn't suspect him of plotting a crime against Jeff? I tried to smile, but my face felt stiff.

"Oh, Mr. Kayro. How are you doing?"

"Just fine." His voice was Peter Lorre's whisper, and his eyes were the size of tennis balls. "Is your weather always this lovely in west Michigan?"

"Now and then we have a blizzard. But have you seen Jeff?"

"Jeff?" Kayro stopped abruptly. "Has he shown up?"

"Yes. He's been discharged from the hospital, and he's here." I smiled. "Or mostly here. He had a concussion, and he has big gaps in his memory."

Kayro's eyes widened, and when eyes that are already the size of tennis balls get even wider, the effect is striking.

"Jeff should be in the dealers' area." I gestured toward the door to the auditorium. "It's the room to the left of the foyer."

Kayro's eyes stayed enormous, and he came to a complete halt. "The dealers' room?"

His reaction was fascinating. "That was where he said he'd be. Let's find him." I stepped forward and motioned for Kayro to follow me.

He didn't. He looked at his watch. "Unfortunately," he said, "I can't do that right now. I have to run an errand. But I'll be right back."

He turned back toward the parking lot and walked away rapidly. He called to me over his shoulder, "Right back! Right back! It will only take a few minutes."

My eyes probably got larger than his as I watched him go. I'd run into Noel Kayro several times over the past few days, and each time we met he had emphasized how eager he was to see Jeff. Now, when I told him Jeff was in close proximity, he turned and ran in the other direction.

What was going on?

Kayro's reaction had made me almost worried about what was going on with Jeff and Tess in the dealers' room. But when I went into that room, all seemed to be well.

Jeff was talking to a fan dressed in a trench coat, Tess was selling a blond moll a paperback book with a blond moll on the cover, and Bodyguard Bob was standing against the wall, looking the crowd over.

If there was anything wrong, it was that Jeff looked a bit tired.

I looked his stock over until he and Tess were both through with the fans, then asked how things were going.

Tess answered, and she spoke firmly. "Jeff's tired."

Jeff denied it, but I thought she was right.

"I can stay for a while," I said. "You could take a rest, Jeff."

"No, no. I'm fine."

I looked around the room and saw a sign saying NOW PLAYING. Under it was a big movie poster. "Oh, Jeff! It's *The Big Sleep*! That used to be one of your favorite movies."

"Yeah. Bogart, Bacall, and Philip Marlowe. Hard to beat."

"Well, here's a plan. You and Bob go see it. Tess and I will mind the booth."

It didn't take too much to convince Jeff. I thought that proved he was quite tired. After all, he'd spent the past few days in bed. Just walking around probably took some energy.

It looked as if Tess and I wouldn't have

much to do. As the showing of the classic movie started, much of the crowd left the area. Two not very comfortable folding chairs were behind the small table, and Tess and I sat down.

"Whew!" she said. "I'm surprised at how much business Jeff and I have done. I haven't even had time to visit the ladies' room!"

"Well, go!" I said. "Jeff seems to have marked all his prices plainly. I think I can handle it for a few minutes."

"I'll be right back." She got to her feet and went toward the lobby, where the restrooms were located.

A fan wearing an old-fashioned police uniform came up, and I turned my attention to the box of vintage paperbacks. Together we found three he wanted, and I took his money. Fifteen bucks toward Jeff's booth rental. I glanced at my watch. It had taken me ten minutes to dig through the paperbacks and convince the costumed film fan that he wanted them. But there was no sign of Tess. I would have expected her to get back from the ladies' room more quickly than that. After all, the restrooms were not far away.

Suddenly I was a bit nervous. Then I assured myself that all was well. Tess was probably refreshing her makeup. Combing her hair. Resting her feet. And I shouldn't leave the booth.

Five more minutes went by, and Tess didn't come. My nervousness was growing. Should I call Bodyguard Bob from inside the theater? What would be the point of that? He couldn't go into the ladies' room. Of course, I could go there. But I couldn't leave the booth. I bit a nail and stared toward the main lobby, willing Tess to come into the dealers' room.

It seemed like a gift when Mary Kay McCurley came through the door, apparently checking on how the film festival was going.

I waved when I saw her. "Mary Kay! Can you do me a favor?"

"Sure, especially if it means I can sit down."

I gestured at the empty chair. "Have a seat for as long as you like. I need to run into the ladies' room. Oh, and these are for you." I pulled the small box of truffles I'd brought her out of my purse and shoved it at her ungraciously.

She *oohed*, but I didn't take time to reply. I simply loaded myself onto my crutch and headed for the lobby and the proper door. I shoved it open and rushed inside. And the door banged into Tess.

"Tess!" I said. "Are you all right!"

"Oh, Lee!" Her voice trembled.

Behind her was a slender young woman in a vintage black suit. A black hat with a rather thick veil was tipped over her forehead, almost hiding her eyes and her svelte hairstyle.

But I recognized her. "Oshawna Bridges!"

"Shut up!" Her voice was harsh. And in her hand was an automatic pistol.

Chapter 23

I can now testify to how mesmerizing a gun can be. I looked at the pistol, and I obeyed Oshawna's every command.

She kept her gun low, right in Tess' back and out of sight of any other people. Of course, there weren't many other people around. Nearly all the film fans were in the theater watching Bogart and Bacall.

I tried to remember Aunt Nettie's example, when she had simply told "Wilmer" to stop acting silly the afternoon before. But I wasn't able to do it. I told myself I couldn't endanger Tess. But the actual reason I obeyed Oshawna was that I simply couldn't think straight. I was so mesmerized that I couldn't visualize anything I could do that might help Tess and me.

The boldest thing I did was reach into my pocket. This action made Oshawna poke me in the ribs with her pistol. "Hands where I can see them," she said. "No funny business."

I took my hand out of my pocket, fast. I hadn't found anything more helpful than a wadded-up Kleenex anyway.

Oshawna, Tess, and I, clumped together like the closest of friends, walked across the lobby. My crutch thumped, but I kept up. I longed to see Bodyguard Bob come out of the theater, but he didn't.

When we reached the front door, Tess shoved it open. We walked across a slab of concrete that formed a porch and went down the steps. I had to slow down and hobble, but Oshawna waited patiently.

I went down the steps looking at my feet, but when I reached the drive I looked up. And I was staring straight into the face of Noel Kayro. He was standing beside a large black sedan, holding the door to the backseat open.

His voice was still a Peter Lorre hiss, and he smiled a Peter Lorre smile. "So you had to bring both of them," he said. "Get into the car, Mrs. Woodyard."

He put his hand in his pocket. Something there pointed at me. Did he have a gun? I wasn't sure, but I decided not to chance it.

Tess and I got into the back, and Oshawna got into the front. She faced backward, kneeling, watching us alertly. The gun was between the front seats, clearly in our sight. But the sedan's side windows were heavily tinted. The interior of the car would only be visible through the windshield. And there was no one in front of the car to look in at us.

Kayro closed the doors with a polite flourish, then went around the car and got into the driver's seat.

I finally spoke, if you can call croaking like a frog speaking. "Where are you taking us?"

"Never mind," Oshawna said. "Do what we say, and you won't get hurt."

Looking back, I again tell myself that I might have done something more assertive, like opening the car door and getting out, but Tess had my right arm in a death grip. Maybe that's only an excuse. Maybe I couldn't do anything because I was scared spitless.

So Tess and I sat quietly in the backseat while the sedan drove across the grounds of Warner Point. I recognized where we were, of course. I'd become familiar with the whole property before Joe got rid of it, and I recognized our route. I knew that the most secluded space out there was the boathouse, and that was where we were going.

When the original buildings were being planned and built, Joe had told me, his wife and her architects handled everything. The only place Joe had any input was the boathouse. He and an architect — a junior member of the big-name firm that designed the estate — came up with what they considered a prizewinning design. Then the landscape designers carefully hid the boathouse area behind trees and bushes. Men can't admit these things, but I knew the whole episode had hurt Joe's feelings.

Now that Warner Point was a conference center, the boathouse was rarely used, and the whole place was overgrown.

When the sedan stopped, Oshawna ordered Tess and me out of the car, still pointing the gun in our direction, and forced us into the boathouse itself. There we found a power boat, a Bayliner, with two rows of seats. Tess and I were motioned into the backseats.

Motions can be so expressive when they include pointing a gun.

Oshawna got into the front and knelt facing us. "Turn around," she said.

"How?" I said. I tried to sound mystified.

"Don't act stupid! Drop to your knees and put your heads down on the seat."

After Tess and I had obeyed, Oshawna

pulled out a blanket from somewhere and threw it over us. Almost immediately the Bayliner's motor started, and we took off.

It was a miserable ride. I'm not a good sailor. My tummy gets mighty queasy if there are waves. Riding on my knees backward with my head down doesn't help.

I will admit that the thought of jumping overboard did occur to me. Maybe if I grabbed Tess' arm and pulled her along with me, we'd make it. But rapidly following that idea was the recollection that Tess could not swim. No, if I did anything dramatic, such as yanking Tess out of the boat, I'd have to keep hold of her and keep her from sinking. I'm a fair swimmer, though far from expert like Joe and Jeff both, but I didn't think I could keep another person afloat for very long. Even if I shed the boot on my left leg. Especially if someone was shooting at us.

Plus, with the blanket over our heads I had no idea where we were. We might have been in the Warner River, since that was where the boathouse was. Of course, we were traveling faster than was legal in the river, but Oshawna and Kayro were not handicapped by obeying any rules. We might just as well be headed out into Lake Michigan. If we jumped into the river, we'd have weeds and stuff growing on the bottom to contend with. But if the boat got well out into Lake Michigan, we might have to swim several miles to reach shore.

I stayed still.

The ride seemed to go on forever. Eventually the motor became quieter, and I could tell that the boat was slowing. That was when my queasy stomach really began to act up, of course. For a seasick person, there's nothing worse than a boat just sitting there and wallowing around in waves. It got so bad I didn't care if Oshawna shot me. I tossed the blanket back and leaned over the side. What happened next wasn't pretty.

Oshawna didn't shoot me. No, she laughed hysterically. If I had been the one with the gun — but that was just wishful thinking. A person who *laughs* at a fellow human being seasick deserves anything bad that could happen to her.

As soon as I could look up, I did, and over my head I saw a big boat. On the stern were the words "La Paloma." Somehow I wasn't surprised. Stealing Grossmann's boat was barely a crime for Noel Kayro and Oshawna Bridges, considering what they'd already done. And Grossman had already told us he was flying to Buffalo that day, so he wasn't around to object.

Tess and I were hustled out of the boat and onto the swim platform, the aft area used for the convenience of swimmers and water skiers. Then we were hustled past the companionway and into the lower deck.

As I hustled, I tried to scan our surroundings. I saw nothing. We were out in Lake Michigan, far from land. There wasn't a single boat in sight, and we could not see the shore. The sun was still high. Without a GPS or at least a compass, we had no way to tell where we were or even which direction was which.

I did notice that Oshawna had taken off her little veiled hat and had added a scarf to her outfit. Kayro had popped on a ball cap. The new head coverings had made them look like regular boaters as we traveled down the river and out into the lake. They weren't missing a trick.

I had paused, and Oshawna snarled at me. "Get a move on!"

Tess and I kept moving, and we were quickly stashed in one of the crew staterooms. The door slammed, and there we were.

"I suppose that door is locked," I said.

"I noticed a bolt screwed to the doorframe," Tess said. "Outside."

"Good for you! I came right in without

noticing a thing."

"I'm sorry about this, Lee. I guess they think taking me will make it easier to get Jeff."

"I imagine you're right. At any rate, there's no monetary reason to stash me on a yacht. Joe and I barely make the mortgage every month. Unless they simply want me to die a miserable death!"

I hobbled rapidly into an attached bathroom — excuse me, on a boat it's a "head." There I tossed the rest of my cookies.

Once I could manage to get up off my knees, I rinsed my mouth, then found a washrag and washed my face.

"Wow!" I said. "I hope they aim this thing into the waves as quickly as possible, or we'll all have terminal seasickness."

"I've never had motion sickness," Tess said.

"Lucky you. They say you eventually 'find your sea legs.' After a few days. I've never found mine."

I found an easy chair, sat down, and tipped my head back. "I suppose you don't have a cell phone in your bra."

"No."

"Rotten of them to snatch us without giving us time to get our purses. I could sure use a breath mint."

We were both trying to put brave faces on the whole thing, but I'm afraid my voice trembled.

Tess began to roam around the stateroom, but I stayed in my easy chair. For the moment I was queasy, but not actually sick. This made me afraid to move, for fear that movement would change the situation.

I watched Tess prowl. In my depleted state, I couldn't figure out why she was bothering. The room had obviously been prepared for captives. I let my eyes roam around. No knives on the dresser waiting for Oshawna and Noel to come in so we could attack them. No way to sabotage the boat's motor. No clubs, guns, or other defensive weapons. No battering rams we could use to knock the door down.

Tess was being more aggressive than I was. At least she was exploring her surroundings, trying to figure out how to do something about our situation. I simply sat like a lump, a miserable lump with a washing machine agitator in my tum.

In a few minutes, however, my stomach settled to a dull swish, and I also began to think about our situation.

Desperate. That was our situation. I fought down panic. There was no reason for Kayro and Oshawna to let us go. If their plan didn't go well, they could simply shove us overboard and forget we had ever existed. If we were lucky, our bodies would drift onto one of west Michigan's beautiful beaches in a couple of weeks.

My middle grew turbulent again. I got up and once more hobbled into the head. How wonderful that we had it!

When I came out, Tess greeted me with a finger to her lips. "Shhh." The sound was very quiet. She came to my side and murmured softly, "Keep quiet. If I put my ear against the wall under that vent, I can hear them talking. That might mean they can hear us."

I hobbled over to the spot she indicated and put my ear against the wall.

But I didn't hear voices. I heard the roar of a boat's motor.

I nearly screamed. Were we pulling out? But the boat we were on kept pitching in the same pattern.

"It's the Bayliner," I said, keeping my voice to a whisper. "One of them has left the yacht. Maybe both of them."

Tess and I monitored the area near the vent, but for more than an hour we heard not a sound. Then we heard the motor boat returning. Tess and I stayed at our listening post, but we heard nothing but steps and faraway voices.

Then the noises were outside our own door. Guiltily we jumped away from the vent. I fell onto the bed and tried to look as if I'd been napping. Tess sat in a chair and stared as the door swung open.

Jeff stood in the doorway.

Chapter 24

We shouldn't have been surprised. After all, Tess and I both knew that Jeff was the point of all this, not us.

Jeff didn't say anything or change his expression. I gasped. And Tess said, "Oh, Jeff! Honey!"

Then the door slammed. Tess threw herself against it. "Jeff!" She began to sob.

I put my ear against the door, and I shushed Tess. When she toned the bawling down slightly, I was able to hear Jeff say angrily, "You said you'd let them go!"

Oshawna gave her evil laugh, and there was no more talking.

Tess was crying harder than ever. *You're the adult,* I reminded myself.

Luckily there was a box of Kleenex in our little head, so I was able to get Tess to blow her nose and wipe her eyes. By appealing to her pride, I was able to get her to stop sobbing.

Since we were still afraid Kayro and Oshawna could hear us, I whispered to her, "Why do you think Jeff is here?"

"They caught him somehow." Sniff, snuff.

"He sounded as if he came willingly. Don't you think he's making some sort of heroic gesture designed to get us released?"

"Oh!" That made her howl again.

"Think, Tess! If he's being brave for you, you've got to be brave for him."

Nod. Sniff, snuff.

"So let's be quiet, absolutely quiet, and keep listening by the vent."

For the next hour we did that. And we didn't hear anything but distant voices.

Then I caught several words. "Is it time?" Kayro said.

"Six thirty. That's five thirty in Dallas."

"Okay. Here goes."

The two of them must have been right over our heads. We could hear them fairly clearly.

"It's Noel." Pause. I realized that his accent was gone. He was speaking like a normal person, not like Peter Lorre.

"Yes, it's me," he said. "We had a problem, but everything went okay. We've got Jeff, plus his little girlfriend and his tall pal, Lee."

Pause. "Don't get your undies in a knot! That's the only way we could get Jeff. But we've got him. Now it's up to you to make the call."

Another pause.

"Sure the money will be for all three of them." Pause. "Write it on your script. Call us as soon as you've talked to his old man. We're relying on you to handle everything smoothly."

Tess and I didn't hear anything else for a while. We sat by the vent, worrying and hearing an occasional far-off sound. And all that happened was it got dark. We turned on the lights beside the beds. Hours and hours had gone by, and we were still prisoners.

My stomach still felt queasy, and I sat in my chair again. But I kept scanning the stateroom. There simply had to be a way to get out of it. But I couldn't think of one.

Of course, if another boat were to come alongside . . . I shook my head. The way things were going, the other boat would probably be full of unarmed pacifists who had just run out of gasoline and couldn't even speed away.

How about the head? I'd read books in which people broke through into the plumbing and escaped from rooms that way.

I forced myself to my feet, went into the bathroom, and looked all around. Nothing but tile. I knelt on the floor, where I'd already spent a lot of time being miserable, and looked at the walls close to the floor. My grandmother's house in Texas had panels here and there in the bathroom walls. They gave access for working on the plumbing. Nothing like that was available in the yacht's head.

I looked in the cupboards, making sure their walls and ceilings had no access to secret passages. Ha. Then I tottered into the bedroom and repeated the process in the cupboards and the one closet there. Again, nothing.

Could we break a hole in the wall? We'd need an ax, a saw, and a crowbar. And we'd bring all the crooks down to see what the noise was.

If we couldn't go through the windows or the walls, we'd just have to go through the door. I hobbled over to the door, knelt, and looked the handle over.

Tess had said there was a bolt on the outside. It wasn't visible to us. And the door opened *into* the room. That meant we couldn't knock it down by throwing ourselves against it. That idea was laughable anyway. Tess and I could bruise ourselves from top to toe and not break that door down. And none of the furniture was heavy enough to make a dent in that metal door.

I fought panic again. It was going to take a miracle to get us out.

Then something happened that seemed almost like a miracle.

First we heard some clicking from outside. Then the door swung open.

We both jumped to our feet, and I moved back from the door. Hope sprang to life. Then I saw that Kayro and Oshawna were outside. And Oshawna was still holding her pistol.

By then I was feeling positive that Kayro had been faking having a pistol in the car. It was interesting that Oshawna always had a pistol, and Kayro didn't. Also interesting that I sensed he was afraid of her.

Kayro was once again wearing his Peter Lorre outfit, and Oshawna was dolled up with the dark ringlets she had worn at Valk Memorabilia, plus the veiled hat.

"Come along," Kayro said. He motioned for us to follow him. "Just remember to obey orders, if you please."

We followed. Kayro, then Tess, then me, then Oshawna and her gun. Kayro led us into the small lower-deck salon, then up a companionway to the larger salon on the next level. The whole rear wall of that salon was glass, and the yacht's garage, on the lower deck, was clearly visible in daylight or if the outside lights were on.

The "garage" on a big pleasure boat is always a showpiece. It's the place where swimmers can dive, where Ski-Doos are launched, and where boats are tied up, then hauled aboard. It's for the storage and use of water toys. Of course, at that moment it was nighttime, and the large glass doors across the back were nothing but a massive reflection. I could barely see that the garage existed.

Jeff was in the salon, facing aft. He was sitting in a chair with wooden arms and legs and a well-padded seat and back. The chair looked comfortable, but Jeff didn't. His fists were clenched, and his arms were tied to the chair's arms.

Tess and I were told to sit in similar chairs next to Jeff. We were fastened to the arms with handcuffs — one pair each. Apparently being forced to add me to the ménage had left the kidnap team short of equipment. They'd had to tie Jeff up.

"Now, we're going to Skype," Kayro said. "We'll be talking to Jeff's dad in a minute. But none of you is to say anything unless you're instructed to. No noise! No sudden moves. I assure you that Rich Godfrey would be most horrified and shocked to see his son, his ex-wife, or his young friend Tess die in front of his very eyes. And that's what will happen if you disobey."

A sheet now hung at one end of the room, behind Jeff, Tess, and me. It would, I realized, stop Rich from seeing any portion of the room we were in. He would have no idea we were on a boat.

The three of us were seated close together, and as they began to work on the computer hookup, Jeff nudged me with his elbow. I looked at him. He looked at his wrist. I looked at his wrist.

The rope holding his wrist was loose. It looked as if it was tied, but I could see he would be able to yank his hand out.

My heart gave a great leap, but I managed not to gasp. Somehow — I'd guess during the time Oshawna and Kayro were bringing Tess and me up — he had managed to loosen one of his wrists.

But what good would one free hand do? I had one free hand, but if I tried to do anything with it, I'd have to drag a chair along.

"Remember! No talking!" Oshawna said.

I didn't like to think about that Skype to Rich. Like the rest of us, he was trying to be brave. It was heartbreaking to see him try to look firm.

And I couldn't believe the ridiculous amount of money they were asking for the three of us.

"I don't have that much money!" Rich said. "If I sold everything I own, I couldn't raise that. Raising half of it would take weeks!"

"According to the *Dallas Morning News* you can raise it," Oshawna said. She and Kayro were off to the side, out of camera range. But she held a newspaper page in front of the camera. Later I saw it. The main article cited Rich as among Dallas' most successful real estate investors. It speculated about him taking his company public and stressed that he was currently sole owner.

Jeff, Tess, and I all kept our mouths shut, as instructed. The only remark came when Oshawna made some taunting comment, asking Jeff if he didn't want to make a plea to his dad.

Jeff shot her a look that should have left her dead, dead, dead. "No," he said.

The call was over soon, with a curt "You'll receive instructions for how to deliver the money" from Oshawna.

The woman then stood before Tess and me. She spoke to Kayro. "Okay. Bring the keys."

He hastened to obey. Again I felt sure that

Oshawna was in charge. "Yes, yes." He used his Peter Lorre voice.

Kayro unlocked our handcuffs.

Oshawna motioned with her pistol. "Back downstairs," she said.

I tried to look pitiful, and I spoke weakly. "Do you have a box of crackers?"

"Crackers!" Her reply was angry.

"Sometimes dry crackers help this miserable motion sickness."

Oshawna laughed. I'd noticed that every time she laughed, she threw her head back and her eyes became slits. "Oh, we won't starve you!"

She stepped back and motioned with the gun. "Follow Kayro."

Tess and I got to our feet. She hung back, trying to see Jeff, but I pushed her ahead. Kayro led. Tess followed him, with me behind her, and Oshawna behind me.

"Single file, Indian-style," Oshawna said sarcastically. We walked to the companionway that led downstairs and started down it. I held my crutch in my right hand, held the railing with my left, and hopped.

Kayro was nearly to the bottom when I retched. I stopped on the second step, turned sideways, and looked back toward Oshawna. I gave her another piteous look and retched again.

And she laughed. She threw her head back, her eyes became slits, and she laughed the way I had known she would.

Putting all my strength into it, I used my crutch like a pool cue and jabbed her in the midriff.

Chapter 25

Everything happened at once.

Oshawna doubled up, tripped on the companionway step, and landed flat on her back at the top of the companionway.

The pistol went off. But nobody yelled, "I'm shot!"

Tess — bless her heart! — jumped onto Kayro's back and grabbed him around the neck. They went down in a heap at the foot of the companionway.

Jeff leaped to his feet and ran toward us, slinging his chair aside. Thank God he'd been able to untie the other hand.

I guess I ran up the three steps to the top of the companionway and stomped on Oshawna's arm with my boot. At least that was the position in which I found myself. I have no recollection now of how I got there, but there I was.

I do remember taking a deep breath and dropping to my knees with one knee on

Oshawna's chest and one on her right wrist. She was still gripping the pistol, but my left knee was keeping her hand immobilized.

"Jeff! Grab the gun!"

"I have to help Tess!"

"Get the gun first!"

Jeff grabbed it, almost casually. Then he did something I hadn't expected at all. He jumped over me and slid down the banister. Don't ask me how anybody who isn't an acrobat could do that. All I knew was I nearly lost my grip on Oshawna as he went over my head.

Then I looked over my shoulder, and Oshawna struck. My crutch had landed on the floor near her left side. She was able to grab it, and she did her best to brain me.

The crutch went by my head closer than Jeff had gone, and I lost hold of her right arm. She pushed me aside and got to her feet. I grabbed her around the knees and clutched the banister to keep the two of us from flying down to the lower deck. But she slithered out of my grip and started running down the stairs.

When I turned to follow her, things had changed, and I immediately ducked. Jeff now had Kayro pinned down, and Tess had the pistol.

"Stop!" Tess yelled. "Stop or I'll shoot!"

Everything froze. Jeff had Kayro immobilized, but he couldn't let go of him. Tess was facing Oshawna, and Oshawna, halfway down the steps, was facing Tess. Neither of them seemed to know what to do. I was holding my breath.

We all stood there, paralyzed, for five or ten seconds. Then I reached for Oshawna and yanked the crutch out of her hand. I had a strong impulse to use it like a baseball bat and hit her upside the head.

Unfortunately I didn't. My inaction was unlucky because she began to talk.

"You are too sweet to kill anybody, darling Tess." Her tone made it clear that her comment was not a compliment. "You are just too, too adorable. Everybody loves you. You're a regular baby doll."

And Oshawna stepped down one step.

"Stop where you are," Tess said.

"Oh, I'm not in any danger, little darling. You couldn't hurt me. It would be completely out of character for the office darling, the campus sweetheart, little Miss Sunshine, the Moonlight Queen to *hurt* anyone."

Tess looked crushed, and I'd had enough. "If you keep talking like that," I said, "I personally *will* kill you." I hefted the crutch. "Start walking! Go down the hallway to the room where you locked Tess and me up. Tess! Get set. If she makes a wrong move, shoot her!"

I guess I'd goaded Oshawna too far. Because she did move.

She jumped at Tess. The pistol went off, but Oshawna had already knocked it up. She was able to get inside Tess' reach and grab the smaller girl.

We were all screaming, God knows what.

I remember shrieking, "Drop the gun! Drop the gun!"

I think Jeff was hollering something like "Get her, Lee!" and I tried to do that. I reached the foot of the stairway somehow, and I tried to hit Oshawna. But there was no way to hit her and not hit Tess.

Finally I did hit Tess. I cracked her wrist with the crutch, and she dropped the pistol. I kicked it under a couch and felt great satisfaction. Then I once again began to whack at Oshawna with my crutch. And, yes, I immediately hit Tess by accident.

If my misplaced blow to Tess had anything to do with what happened next, I will never admit it. But suddenly Oshawna broke free.

She looked wildly around the room and shouted, "Where's the gun?"

I shouted back, "Overboard!"

Oshawna growled. Actually growled like

an animal. Then she whirled toward the aft deck and ran to the giant double doors that connected to the deck above the garage. I was hobbling after her, and Tess was coming, too. Oshawna shoved one of the sliding doors open. She ran outside full tilt.

But Tess wasn't giving up. She dove at Oshawna and got her arms around her waist. Oshawna didn't stop. She kept going, ricocheted into the rail, and tumbled over it.

She dragged Tess along. They hit the lower deck and bounced off the stern of the yacht and into Lake Michigan.

I heard a loud roar behind me, and Jeff went by me. He stood at the railing, looking down, and yanking off his clothes. Shoes and pants flew into the air.

"Tess! Tess!" he yelled. "I'm coming to get you."

"Get a life ring!" I was yelling louder than he was.

Jeff went over the side, right into the pitch-black waters of Lake Michigan.

I ran to the aft rail and stared into the dark. I didn't know if I should cry, scream, or jump in myself. I was now alone on an enormous boat — with one of the crooks.

Kayro could be coming toward me, ready

to throw me after the others. I whirled around.

But no. He was still lying on the floor in the lower deck lounge. I could barely see him because a large sofa was on top of him.

"May I please get up?" he said.

"Not until I find someone stronger than I am to turn that couch back over," I said.

Then I ran to the couch where I had kicked the gun, dropped to my stomach, and fished it out. I went back to Kayro. "Where can I find lights for the swim platform?"

"Back by the garage. On the right-hand wall."

But when I went back to the garage I saw lights, not on the yacht, but out on the water. And a searchlight hit me.

A boat was coming toward us. I waved frantically. Then I stopped. How did I know I wanted that boat to find me? It seemed as if the whole world was full of bad guys. The boat coming near might simply be more of them.

There was a companionway from the main deck down to the swim platform, naturally. I took it without even thinking about needing a crutch.

I yelled into the dark, "Jeff! Tess!"

I turned on the lights that Kayro had

described, and I used them to find *La Paloma*'s searchlight. I moved it back and forth over the water. But I saw no one. I found the ladder swimmers used to climb into the boat. I made sure it was accessible. I would have jumped in and tried to save one of them — Jeff, Tess, or even Oshawna. But I couldn't see any of them.

"Oh, God," I prayed, "don't let Jeff and Tess drown. Don't even let Oshawna drown."

Then I turned to look at the oncoming boat. I made "go slow" signals. With swimmers in the water — well, it was a dangerous situation.

When I turned back to the swimmer's ladder, a hand was gripping it.

I screamed and ran over to it. And another hand appeared.

Tess flew onto the ramp, pushed aboard by unseen hands. "Don't shove!" she said. "I can climb in myself!"

Jeff yanked himself onto the ramp beside her. They both lay on the swim platform, panting.

I'd been hugging them for at least two minutes before either of them had the strength to talk. Then it was Jeff.

"Lee, I'm not sure I want to marry Tess after all."

"After you pulled her out of Lake Michigan?"

"I didn't pull her out! She pulled herself out. All this time she's told me she never learned to swim! And she swims like a catfish!"

Tess was on her knees by then, still panting. "You love swimming so much I got determined I was going to learn. I was the only senior in the beginners' class! And I made an A! I was going to surprise you and show off the first time we were around a pool!"

That was when the bullhorn began to blare, "Coming aboard! Warner Pier Police! Coming aboard."

It was Hogan. But he wasn't the first person who came aboard. That was Joe. He jumped onto the yacht before the frogmen could get there.

I was sure glad to see him. I gave him a big hug.

Then I ran for the railing.

Chapter 26

The coast guard and the Michigan State Police sent boats to join the search for Oshawna. Their efforts were useless. Her body washed up near Holland five days later.

Except for a bad bruise on her arm, probably made by my crutch, Tess was unharmed by her fall from one deck to the other and her dunking in Lake Michigan. And his swim in the cold, dark waters seemed to invigorate Jeff. He sounded tip-top as he called his parents to report on our escape.

We headed back to Warner Pier, with Joe at the helm of the yacht and one of the Warner Pier Police boat volunteers as crew. Joe wasn't even pretending not to be enjoying his temporary status as "captain" of the beautiful yacht. The phrase "basking in it" comes to mind.

Noel Kayro, of course, had been shifted to the police boat, which had a place to lock him up. I was still feeling queasy and sat in an easy chair in the main salon, ready to jump for a nearby head. Tess was wrapped in a blanket and stretched out on a couch with her head in Jeff's lap.

"It's a miracle you didn't break a leg when you fell onto the swim platform," I said.

"I managed to land on top of Patsy," she said. "She finally did me a favor."

"Patsy? Oshawna's real name is Patsy?"

Tess nodded.

"And how did you know that?" I asked.

"I've known Patsy since my freshman year," Tess said. "Jeff met her, too. She and I were in the same dorm. Recently she worked for Jeff's dad."

"Patsy!" I finally got it. "Alicia told me you had a friend in Michigan named Patricia."

"Not a friend," Tess said.

"Alicia said you got Patsy a job," I said.

"I found Patsy when Alicia needed someone in a hurry."

"But you weren't friends?"

"Patsy and I knew each other, but we were basically enemies. In fact, I've been wondering if this whole thing started because she couldn't stand me. She made a big play for Jeff our sophomore year."

"She did not!" Jeff said.

"She did, too!" Tess glared at him.

I decided to head off that little tiff. "But you still helped her get a job?"

"Oh, sure. She needed money, and Alicia needed a receptionist." Tess' eyes got wide. "I wasn't trying to play up to Patsy! It just happened. And I bet she got a lot of information about Jeff and his family by working there. Such as when the boss and his wife would be back from Peru. You know office gossip."

"But why didn't you tell us who she was earlier?"

"I never saw her until she waylaid me in the ladies' room, Lee. She was able to fool Jeff because he hadn't seen much of her in a couple of years. And she was great at makeup and changing her appearance. I think she deliberately dodged me up here, because I would have known her in any disguise. Then, after we were kidnapped, I didn't say anything because I thought it was smarter to pretend I didn't recognize her."

Tess sat up and looked at me with tears in her eyes. "I'd hate to think anybody hated me so much that they caused all this trouble — and that people actually died because of our feud."

"I think Oshawna — or Patsy — was responsible for causing her own and other people's problems. You can't blame yourself."

Tess looked uncertain. "I don't know."

"I guess I don't know either. But I feel too rotten to discuss philosophy." I ran for the head again. And when I came out, Tess and I dropped that subject.

"I wish Hogan was on this boat," she said. "I've got some questions I hope he can answer."

"He's probably too busy tonight. What do you want to ask him?"

"Why on earth Captain Jacobs brought that worthless falcon to your house."

"I'd like to know what you did with it. And why."

"Oh. I sent it to myself at your house, by UPS." Tess hung her head. "Sort of like Sam Spade did when he put the falcon in a locker and mailed the key. It seemed like a good idea at the time. But why did the captain even have it?"

"I don't know," I said. "I wonder if Hogan can explain who was in Dallas."

"Whom do you mean?"

"Oshawna and Kayro called somebody down there, somebody who was to contact Jeff's folks and pick up the ransom. Who was that?"

"I can take a guess," Jeff said. "I think it

might have been Hal. Hal Hale."

"But isn't Kayro Hal?"

Jeff shook his head. "No, he isn't. At least he's not the Hal I worked with at the museum. I don't know who this Kayro guy is."

There were other questions, but at that point Joe gave a loud whistle from the bridge, and we all looked at him. "Lighthouse ho!" he said. "If I've aimed this thing right, we're coming up on the Warner River. Prepare for a joyful homecoming."

Joyful was right, at least for me. As any sufferer from motion sickness can testify, as soon as you stop moving, you're okay. The smooth ride up the river settled my innards, and walking across the gangway at the marina completed the cure. I didn't kiss the ground, but I sure was tempted.

Hogan promised to meet everyone for brunch the next morning and answer any questions he could. "I don't have all the answers yet," he said. "I'm guessing at a lot of it."

The next morning we gathered in the private room at the Sidewalk Café, one of Joe's stepfather's restaurants. After indulging in omelets, pancakes, bacon, and other goodies, all of us stared at Hogan, ready to hear the story.

They had identified the participants as Patsy Parker, whose pseudonym was Oshawna Bridges; Hal Hale, who had volunteered with Jeff at the Dallas museum, and Linwood Yardley, who at noir events went by Noel Kayro.

In a phone call Grossman had told Hogan that Yardley was a sort of manager for his yacht. He was not a licensed captain, but made sure that the vessel had a proper crew, ordered supplies, and took care of other details for Grossman. He had sailed on the yacht often, Grossman said, and was perfectly capable of taking her on short trips.

His full-time job, Grossman said, was as a professional researcher. Jeff had been perfectly right about Grossman. He didn't know squat about noir, because he didn't do his own research. He just parroted what Yardley told him.

"Research apparently doesn't pay much," Hogan said to us. "Grossman hired him to work on the yacht part-time because he looked so much like that actor Peter Lorre. His job included assisting Grossman at conventions where he was speaking."

Patsy, Hal, and Kayro met at a film noir convention in San Antonio, perhaps drawn by Hal's and Kayro's resemblance to each other, as well as to Peter Lorre. Patsy was earning a little extra money at the event by doing makeup for fans who wanted to look like Hammett characters.

It was Patsy who mentioned a fellow noir fan in Dallas who came from a wealthy family and who, or so she thought, would be easy to entice with a con job. Hogan was tactful enough not to use the word "innocent" in front of Jeff. No twenty-two-year-old guy likes to be accused of being innocent.

Hal and Yardley liked the idea. A plot was born.

Bur Jeff was, after all, a history major, and the three plotters had underestimated his ability as a researcher. He scoffed at their initial attempt at a con job, the Mary Astor pendant. Unwilling to abandon their plan, Patsy, Kayro, and Hal considered kidnapping him. At this point Patsy revealed that she was one of several cousins who had inherited a cabin deep in the woods of Michigan. A cabin not currently occupied.

The perfect place to keep a kidnap victim.

Patsy also kept track of Jeff's parents through office gossip. If they were out of the country, for example, Jeff would not be able to ask for money to buy falcon items. But they had to be back in time to pay his ransom.

But the plotters had to come up with something that would attract Jeff to Michigan. And they'd have to convince him he should keep his trip secret. Scanning the Internet, Hal discovered our Warner Pier Film Festival. He was relieved to learn Jeff was interested in going. Kayro urged Grossman, his boss, to offer a big prize for information on a third Maltese Falcon. Apparently Grossman really believed Kayro's story of a possible third falcon.

At the same time, Hal and Kayro began corresponding with Jeff, pretending to represent the fictional "Falcone Memorabilia." Jeff kept quiet about the possibility of a third falcon, mainly because he doubted it existed. But if it did, he wanted to profit from it himself.

Then the conspirators made a big mistake. They assumed that Jeff was in Dallas and would meekly stay there until they invited him to visit Falcone's in Michigan. They thought it would take at least three days for him to drive to Michigan and then he'd need directions to their remote location.

Actually Jeff had already left for Michigan, thinking he'd see Joe, Aunt Nettie, Hogan, and me before the film festival began.

And by quizzing the Dorinda postmaster he figured out how to reach Falcone's on his own initiative, then simply got in his car and drove out there. He arrived days before Patsy and Kayro were ready to imprison him.

When he approached the cabin in the woods, no one was there but Patsy. And she couldn't get to her gun.

Patsy, in her Oshawna persona, could not convince Jeff he should stay around long enough for Kayro to help her imprison him.

As Jeff drove off, she followed him out to Lake Shore Drive. At a deserted spot less than a mile from our house, she forced his car off the road. Jeff's head hit the windshield, but he managed to hide in the bushes, then reach our house. Confused by his injury, he climbed into the attic and passed out.

Meanwhile, Patsy and Kayro moved Jeff's car miles away from the scene of his crash and tried to hide it in heavy woods.

Again the conspirators thought they would have to give up the plot to kidnap Jeff. They thought he was probably dead.

Patsy and Kayro searched desperately for Jeff. Joe and I came across them at the Holiday Inn Express, where Kayro was checking in. He overheard me telling the manager that Jeff had been in an accident and was hospitalized. Meanwhile Patsy, disguised as Wilmer, tried to get into Jeff's room. Apparently she was noisy about it; the woman across the hall complained, to us and to the front desk.

Patsy also tried to find Jeff in the hospital, but because Jeff had been admitted as "J. R. Ewing," rather than under his own name, she couldn't find him.

Then the yacht's captain, Jacobs, blundered onto the plot. Or that was what Hogan believed. "He figured out something was wrong," he said. "Maybe he eavesdropped. Or maybe it was the bolt on the outside of the stateroom door. That pretty much indicated someone was going to be locked inside."

Jeff spoke. "I've never understood why he took that silly fake falcon."

"You forget that everybody doesn't know as much about the *Maltese Falcon* as you do, Jeff. Jacobs just signed on for the trip. He may have thought the falcon was real. The question is, why did he think he should take it to Joe?"

Joe nodded. "All I can think is that I may have made some comment about the police chief being a relative. That's pretty far-fetched, but it's all I've come up with. Anyway, I guess it's definite that Oshawna — Patsy — shot him. We didn't hear the shot, so he must have walked quite a way before he reached our house."

I tried not to think about that. Poor guy.

When Jeff had finally come out in public, he had a bodyguard, making it hard for the kidnappers to approach him. Improvising, Patsy and Kayro kidnapped Tess, taking me along because I stumbled onto the scene.

Just as it became clear that Tess and I were missing, Patsy walked through the theater's lobby and left Jeff a note. "Come along with me, or Tess and Lee are dead."

Jeff didn't hesitate. He was brave, but maybe not too smart. He waited until Bodyguard Bob went into a stall in the men's room, then jammed the door shut and split. But he wasn't completely stupid. He had taken Tess' bug from his car that morning. For his kidnapping, he put the thing in his pocket with his cell phone. Even when the crooks took the cell phone away from him, they missed the bug.

"It took me a little while to catch on," Hogan said, "but we were able to follow the signal. We knew where he was pretty soon."

The coast guard used their radar to help locate *La Paloma* in the right area, and Hogan and his crew, with backup from the Michigan State Police, headed out in the Warner Pier Police boat, a vessel they own primarily for more ordinary boating emergencies.

Hogan smiled. "Thanks to the kidnapped people turning on the kidnappers . . ."

"And Lee hitting Oshawna with her crutch!" Tess said.

"And Jeff chewing his ropes off!" I said.

"And Tess bulldogging Kayro!" Jeff said.

"Anyway," Hogan said, "I'm not a praying man, I'm afraid, but we all ought to be down on our knees."

There was a long moment of silence. And I think quite a few prayers were flying upward.

Then Joe spoke. "And now we've got to head for the airport."

We ran for the cars. Rich had called early that morning, reporting that he'd borrowed a business jet from a friend. He, Dina, Buck, and Tess' mom, Marie, would be arriving in Grand Rapids in about an hour.

It was hard to get a room in Warner Pier when the film festival was on. Buck, Marie, and Tess were going to stay with us, and Jeff, Rich, and Dina with Aunt Nettie and Hogan. My tactful Aunt Nettie had arranged all that. I wasn't quite ready to have Rich staying in my house, and I didn't think Joe was either.

Tess had already changed the sheets on

the upstairs beds. I gave her two sets, but she brought down only one, saying, "I don't mind sleeping on Jeff's sheets." I didn't say anything, but she blushed anyway.

After all Tess' talk about how tough her dad was, I was amazed and amused when he got off the Learjet.

The rough, tough, manly Buck Riley was five feet two inches tall and weighed about a hundred pounds. My Texas grandmother would have called him a "banty rooster." My Michigan grandmother might have called him that, too.

But as soon as he shook hands with Hogan he said, "I reckon you're a pretty smart lawman. Believe me, Marie and I will never forget what all y'all hev done for our little girl."

"She did a lot for herself, Buck," Hogan said. "She's not one to sit on her hands and let people push her around."

"She'd better not be!" Buck said. "I tried to teach all those kids to stand up for the'selves. But what you did saved me a prison term. Because believe me, I woulda killed anybody who hurt her."

Marie stepped up at that. "Now, Buck," she said, managing to give his name two syllables. "Don't start tellin' people how you'd run things till you've been here a day or two. And it won't hurt you to tip the luggage fellow."

I loved Buck. He was just like a trip home. I like Michigan fine, but there's nowhere like Texas.

Rich had arranged to be met by a rental car, and Tess said her parents could use hers.

So Joe and I drove back to Warner Pier alone.

"Whew!" he said. "Is the end of the Texas invasion in sight?"

"Nope. Even if all this bunch goes home, I'm staying."

"Good enough. I couldn't get along without you. So git out yore hat!" He patted my knee and pointed to my orthopedic boot. "You've already got a boot!"

"I guess that turned out to be a good thing."

"I never thought I'd be glad you sprained an ankle. And I sure didn't visualize a crutch as a defensive weapon."

CHOCOLATE CHAT

Another interesting fudge recipe comes from Eagle Brand Sweetened Condensed Milk.

Chocolate Fudge

3 cups (18 ounces) semisweet chocolate chips

1 14-ounce can of Eagle Brand Sweetened Condensed Milk or Eagle Brand Fat-Free Sweetened Condensed Milk

dash salt

1 1/2 teaspoons vanilla extract

Line 8- or 9-inch pan with waxed paper. Melt chocolate chips with sweetened condensed milk and salt in a heavy saucepan. Remove from heat. Stir in vanilla. Spread evenly in prepared pan. Chill two hours, or until firm. Remove from pan by lifting edges of waxed paper, then peeling off paper. Cut into squares.

ABOUT THE AUTHOR

Eve K. Sandstrom is the real name for novelist JoAnna Carl. Eve was born in Oklahoma; she spends her time living between Oklahoma and Michigan. Her popular Chocoholic Series is set in a West Michigan resort town.

The employees of Thorndike Press hope you have enjoyed this Large Print book. All our Thorndike, Wheeler, and Kennebec Large Print titles are designed for easy reading, and all our books are made to last. Other Thorndike Press Large Print books are available at your library, through selected bookstores, or directly from us.

For information about titles, please call:

(800) 223-1244

or visit our Web site at:

http://gale.cengage.com/thorndike

To share your comments, please write:

Publisher
Thorndike Press
10 Water St., Suite 310
Waterville, ME 04901